D0523724

SPECIAL MESSAGE TO READERS

THE ULVERSCROFT FOUNDATION
(registered UK charity number 264873)
was established in 1972 to provide funds for research, diagnosis and treatment of eye diseases. Examples of major projects funded by the Ulverscroft Foundation are:-

- The Children's Eye Unit at Moorfields Eye Hospital, London
- The Ulverscroft Children's Eye Unit at Great Ormond Street Hospital for Sick Children
- Funding research into eye diseases and treatment at the Department of Ophthalmology, University of Leicester
- The Ulverscroft Vision Research Group, Institute of Child Health
- Twin operating theatres at the Western Ophthalmic Hospital, London
- The Chair of Ophthalmology at the Royal Australian College of Ophthalmologists

You can help further the work of the Foundation by making a donation or leaving a legacy. Every contribution is gratefully received. If you would like to help support the Foundation or require further information, please contact:

THE ULVERSCROFT FOUNDATION
The Green, Bradgate Road, Anstey
Leicester LE7 7FU, England
Tel: (0116) 236 4325

website: www.foundation.ulverscroft.com

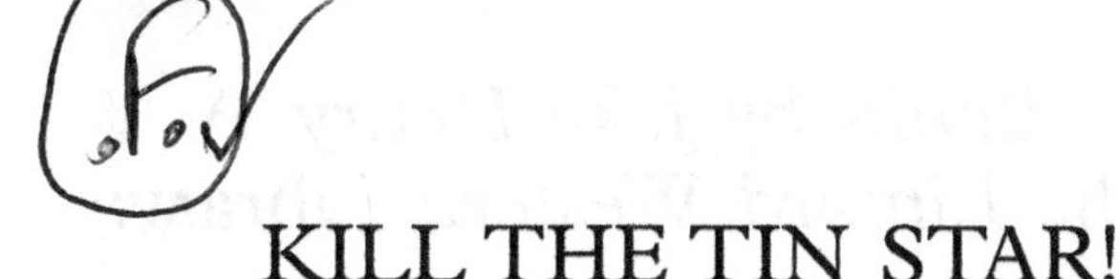

KILL THE TIN STAR!

They warned Savage not to take the short cut through Dead Man's Gulch. Too many Apaches, they said. The warning, however, failed to mention anything about Craig and Bobby Vandal. Father and son. One a cold killer, the other prepared to do anything for his boy. When Savage arrives in the Gulch, the local sheriff has Bobby locked up on a murder charge. Craig swears his son will never hang. Before long, a deputy's badge is pinned to Savage's chest, and he holds a smoking-hot Winchester in his hands . . .

Books by Jake Henry
in the Linford Western Library:

SAVAGE
A GUN FOR SHELBY

JAKE HENRY

KILL THE TIN STAR!

Complete and Unabridged

LINFORD
Leicester

First published in Great Britain in 2017

First Linford Edition
published 2018

*A catalogue record for this book is available
from the British Library.*

ISBN 978–1–4448–3884–8

Published by
F. A. Thorpe (Publishing)
Anstey, Leicestershire

Set by Words & Graphics Ltd.
Anstey, Leicestershire
Printed and bound in Great Britain by
T. J. International Ltd., Padstow, Cornwall

This book is printed on acid-free paper

This one is for Sam and Jacob.

Prologue

It was called San Vicente. Well, that's what the locals called it at the time. Its full name was *La Ciénega de San Vicente*. Which meant the Marsh of St. Vincent. Its history could be traced back to the arrival of the Spaniards.

In later years, after silver was discovered, the name would change to Silver City. As with many boom towns, violence soon followed and brought death with it.

It would become familiar with the names Harvey Whitehill, William Bonney, and 'Dangerous' Dan Tucker. It would see Indian attacks and come to know the legend of the Lost Adams Diggings.

In 1871, it became the county seat for Grant County and in 1881, the Atchison, Topeka, and Santa Fe Railroad had its terminus there.

But this is not a story about *La*

Ciénega de San Vicente or Silver City.

Nor is it the story of Pinos Altos, a gold town built on Chiricahua land, originally known as Birchville, created as a supply town for miners or a place to get a woman's companionship.

A town that also played host to a man who operated a mercantile before heading to West Texas. His name, Roy Bean.

The Apaches, led by Mangas Coloradas, who along with the great chief, Cochise, banded together and swore to drive the hated white-eyes from the lands that weren't theirs. They only succeeded in making them more determined to stay.

No, this story isn't about any of them. This story is about a town quite similar to those mentioned, further north by ten miles. Founded on the back of a gold strike, it was violent and rugged. Formed by tents and timber structures along a muddy main street.

Surrounded by Apache lands, the miners not only fought each other, but the Chiricahua too. Raids on the town had killed miners, storekeepers, men and women. They came with the dawn and were gone before the mist had lifted, leaving behind death and destruction. After every episode, the whites would rebuild.

Eventually, the Apaches were moved on and the mines ran their course until the ground had nothing more to offer. And so, as mining towns do, this one died, leaving nothing but memories.

Memories of violence, death, and a man called Drifter. The town was called Dead Man's Gulch.

1

When Bobby Vandal strode into the dimly-lit, smoke-filled room of the Down and Out saloon, every person there knew that somebody would die this night. When he started drinking, it was not an unusual outcome, and judging by his altered gait, the suggestion might be that he'd already had quite a few.

The tall, young man bellied up to the rough-built pine bar and slammed his hand down on its top. 'Give me whiskey, damn it!'

A livid scar that ran down his right cheek, puckered as he squinted his ice-blue eyes with the command.

A thin, rat-faced barkeep looked up at Bobby and saw the no-nonsense look on his face and stopped what he was doing. He moved along the bar toward the man, aware of the quiet exodus of customers who wanted nothing to do with Bobby Vandal.

The barkeep reached under the counter and brought up a two-thirds full bottle and a glass. He placed it on the battered counter-top and looked the scarred hellion in the eyes.

'That'll be . . . ' He never finished because Bobby scooped up the bottle and glass and walked away.

He paused after a few steps and looked around the room. He was sure that there had been more people in the saloon when he walked in, and there seemed to be a distinct lack of females plying their trade. He grinned wickedly and settled his gaze on a poker game near the front window.

The players dropped their gazes in the hope that he'd pay them and their game, no further attention. Or maybe they'd get lucky and his Pa would appear and take his trouble-making son home to sober up.

As luck would have it, neither of their hopes were realized that evening and

Bobby Vandal headed in the direction of the table where the four scared men sat.

He stopped beside a rail-thin man with a comb-over and placed his bottle and glass on the tabletop. He put his hand on the card player's shoulder, making him flinch involuntarily.

'Get up,' Bobby said in a low, commanding voice.

Without hesitation, the player leaned forward hurriedly to scoop his winnings and stuff his pockets.

'Leave the money there,' Bobby ordered.

The card player looked over his shoulder at Bobby, a pleading expression upon his face.

'Get up and go!' Bobby commanded again. 'I won't tell you a third time.'

The man moved slowly. He was reluctant to leave upwards of fifty dollars on the table. Then again, he felt the same way about dying. He gave one last wistful look at the money he was forfeiting and walked from the saloon.

Bobby sat down and pulled the money towards himself. He looked around the table at the remaining three men.

'Any objections?' he asked.

As expected, none of them spoke.

Bobby sat down and held out his hand for the deck of cards. The man seated opposite passed them over and the young killer began to shuffle.

'I must warn you,' he stated matter-of-factly as he started to deal, 'I'm a sore loser.'

* * *

Sightless eyes stared at the ceiling as the man lay on his back, a neat hole just above the bridge of his nose, trickling blood. The wall directly behind his position at the game was plastered with a gory mass of bright-red blood, bone chips, and brain matter.

The last two gamblers at the table stared dumbly at the still smoking six-gun in Bobby Vandal's right fist.

'I told you I don't lose good,' he snarled. 'He didn't seem to listen though, did he?'

The dull orange glow of lanterns hung like a shroud across the bar-room. Every customer had backed away from where Bobby Vandal stood, chair tipped on its side. But the two gamblers were trapped. They would go nowhere without the scar-faced killer's say-so.

It hadn't taken long for Bobby to lose patience and kill the man. Four hands had done it. He'd lost every one of them. The dead man had only won one of those but unfortunately, his just happened to be the last one.

On the first hand, all the players tried to fold but Bobby wouldn't let them. They were ordered to play the hands they had. Which meant that the deck was stacked against them from the start.

'There was no need to do that Bobby,' the barkeep called out. 'Hell, it weren't even your money you were losin'.'

'Shut your yap, Roy,' Bobby snarled. 'Unless you want to rest beside our dead friend here?'

The angrier he got, the more the scar on his face stood out against his sun-burnished skin. He was so wrapped up in his latest achievement, that he failed to hear the approach of a man behind him, who said in a menacing tone, 'Drop the gun Bobby or I'll blow your spine in half with this sawn-off I'm holdin'.'

Bobby Vandal stiffened. He thought carefully then said in a loud, clear voice, 'Back off Charley or I'll kill you too.'

Sheriff Charley Halley thumbed the double hammers back on the weapon in his hands. The ratcheting sound seemed almost deafening in the immediate silence.

'Drop it, Bobby.'

Halley was a middle-aged man with graying hair and a lined, walnut-colored face. He had been the local law for almost twelve months and this was just the next in a line of times he'd butted heads with Bobby Vandal.

Each time Bobby had killed, he'd claimed self-defense. This time, however, was different. The dead man didn't have a gun.

'It was self-defense, Charley,' Bobby said, beginning to sing his familiar tune.

'He don't have a gun, Bobby,' Halley pointed out. 'Claimin' that ain't goin' to save you this time. Now I said drop the gun.'

Bobby Vandal was nothing if not persistent.

'My Pa won't stand for it, Charley,' Bobby vowed.

Craig Vandal was the most powerful man in Dead Man's Gulch. He owned the largest gold mine, and was backed by tough guns who ensured that no one got between their boss and what he wanted. He collected taxes from the town's people as protection money because his hired guns acted as a form of security in times of Indian attack.

'He'll take this town apart before he lets me swing rope. He'll kill . . . '

Bobby Vandal never finished. Charley Halley stepped forward and the sawn-off came around in a vicious arc, catching the killer in the back of his head with a solid thwack! Bobby's legs turned to rubber and he collapsed into an untidy heap on the floor of the Down and Out.

A collective sigh sounded as Halley looked about the stunned but relieved group. He picked out two men and said, 'Help me get the jumped-up son of a bitch over to the jail. This time he's goin' to hang for sure.'

* * *

The law of averages said that travelling through Apache territory was not a matter of if, but a matter of when you would come across them. The people in Pinos Altos had warned him that if he continued his current heading, he would eventually find trouble with the

Chiricahua. They advised him to strike directly east and then north to Socorro. A determined Savage ignored their advice and went his own way.

That way was the trail to Dead Man's Gulch but a band of Chiricahua braves were about to have their say on whether he would make it or not.

Savage sat atop his pinto and looked down at the bodies of two miners who lay beside the shallow creek. Their scalps were gone, exposing a dried bloody mess, thick with large black flies. The clothes had been stripped from their bodies and they were staked out, their limbs secured with rawhide thongs to prevent movement while they were worked on with razor-sharp knives.

Both men were missing their eyelids, which had been sliced off neatly. One had been poked in both eyes with a burning stick which left empty blackened sockets. The other miner had his genitals removed and stuffed into his mouth and his stomach had been slashed open and his intestines were piled upon his chest.

Both had died violent, horrible deaths and Savage knew that a similar fate could be his if he wasn't careful.

Savage scanned his surroundings with alert brown eyes, taking in the rough camp. A sluice box was situated by the creek and a stained canvas tent had been set up away from the creek bank in the shade of some tall pines.

The pinto moved nervously and flared its nostrils as the scent of death reached them. Savage patted a reassuring hand on its muscular neck.

He wasn't a big man as such, standing 6-foot-1. His skin was tanned but a heavy stubble obscured the lower part of his face and a low-crowned black hat covered his black hair and forehead. A Union issue shirt and a buckskin jacket covered his solid frame. All, he decided, would be replaced when he hit Albuquerque.

About his waist was a gun belt with loops full of ammunition for his .44

caliber Remington six-gun. In the saddle scabbard was a Winchester rifle, known as the Yellow Boy. It was Winchester's answer to the Henry rifle and it fired a .44 Henry slug.

Off to Savage's left, on the other side of the bubbling creek, a raven took flight with a loud squawk, causing him to take the Yellow Boy from its scabbard. The clack-clack sound of the lever being worked and a round being chambered seemed to echo through the trees.

Savage rested it across his blue-clad thighs and waited patiently for what would happen next. He had briefly considered turning the pinto around and riding hell-for-leather out of there but instantly dismissed the idea. The Apaches were all around him. Five he thought, maybe six. He decided to wait and see.

There was a flicker of movement in the shadows of the tall pines on the far side of the creek. Savage let his eyes dart left and right. He picked up more movement as a dark shape flitted from tree to tree.

The sudden appearance of a Chiricahua beside a tall tree across the creek caused Savage to raise his rifle and sight along the barrel. His finger rested on the trigger but the Indian remained unmoving.

He was dressed in a faded and stained shirt with the sleeves missing, knee-high moccasins, and a loin cloth. About his head was tied a pale bandanna to keep his long black hair away from his face.

Still, the Apache stood there.

It was a hesitation that could have cost Savage his life but a sixth sense told him that all was not right. He swiveled in the saddle and squeezed the trigger as a second Chiricahua on his left was nocking an arrow. The Yellow Boy kicked back against Savage's shoulder and the sound of the shot whiplashed through the surrounding trees.

The bullet punched into the Indian's

chest knocking him back onto his butt, a stunned expression on his face, the arrow flying harmlessly away. Savage levered another round into the breech of the rifle and shifted his aim.

The rifle roared again and an Apache with an old Spencer Carbine had his throat torn open by the Winchester's .44 caliber slug. The brave fell to his knees, his hands reaching up to the ghastly wound, trying to stem the blood flow. He opened his mouth and a flood of crimson liquid cascaded over his chin onto his naked torso. He toppled sideways and died on a bed of thick grass.

Savage worked the lever of the Winchester one more time but held his fire, rifle in his right hand, finger on the trigger. With his left hand, he took up the pinto's reins and gave the animal a brutal kick.

The horse lurched forward and plunged down the bank into the shallow creek, sending up a spray of water as its hoofs ploughed through. Behind him,

Savage heard the blast of a rifle and the crack of the bullet as it passed close to him.

Most people faced with a similar situation would have turned and run. But not Savage.

The sight of the white man riding towards him was not what the Chiricahua was expecting and before the Indian could react, the pinto was almost upon him.

The Apache's eyes grew wide and he hurriedly reached down to draw his knife. Before he could, however, the Yellow Boy discharged no more than a foot from his head.

The bullet smashed the Chiricahua's jaw bone before deflecting up into his brain. He fell into a jumbled heap of arms and legs. Savage kicked the pinto again, urging it to go faster. Behind him, he could hear shouts as the Apaches called out to each other. Off to his right, another Indian appeared from behind a tree.

Savage snapped a shot in that

direction not expecting to hit anything. He saw bark pieces fly from the tree as his bullet ploughed into the soft wood. The shot made the Apache duck reflexively and Savage rode on into the trees. He placed the Winchester back in its scabbard before circling back around to the trail.

Once the pinto hit the path, he pointed it towards Dead Man's Gulch.

More gunfire sounded behind Savage, but he urged the horse on. The beast responded to his rider and lengthened its stride. The rutted trail made a left turn between some rocks but the horse negotiated it with ease.

Farther along, the terrain flattened out and the gunfire behind Savage stopped. He cast a glance over his shoulder and saw three Chiricahua warriors giving chase way back along the trail. Inwardly he cursed himself for disregarding the warnings.

The trail began to climb and ran along a steep-sided ridge with large trees and boulders covering the slopes on each side. Things then went from bad to worse. Coming down the hill towards him was another band of Chiricahua. Maybe six was Savage's guess.

He hauled back on the horse's reins and the animal came to a sliding stop. He turned to look along his backtrail and saw that the others were still in pursuit.

'Shit!' he cursed out loud. 'Serves you damn right for not listening.'

His options had just been halved and of his available remaining choices, neither was appealing.

To his left, the ridge dropped away into a deep ravine. Halfway down, the slope turned into a sheer drop of some thirty feet. On the right, the uneven slope was strewn with trees, deadfalls, and rocks. At the bottom of the descent was a creek.

With one last look left and right, Savage drove his heels into the pinto's flanks and sent it over the edge and on a headlong plunge towards the watercourse at the bottom of the slope.

Leaning back in the saddle, Savage felt every jarring stride as the pinto leapt and slid its way through scree, rocks, and logs on its way towards the creek below.

At the top of the ridge, on the edge of the trail, the Chiricahua brought their horses to a halt and watched in wonder as the crazy white man careened down the dangerous slope and out of sight.

2

When Savage rode into Dead Man's Gulch on a spent horse, he found a transitioning town with canvas structures as well as log buildings along the main street with large false-fronts.

Log houses had been erected by those who'd taken the time to build them, while others, more concerned with finding their fortunes, still lived in single-room canvas abodes.

The hotel was obviously a recently completed double-story construction, its timbers still green. The logs had been harvested from the rapidly receding forest that surrounded the town.

A hit and miss series of boardwalks had been constructed outside of each timber building so when it rained, folks could walk in comfort for the width of the false-fronted building before stepping down into the sucking mud outside of the canvas ones.

Some of the other newly constructed timber buildings were the jail, one of the three saloons, the mercantile, and an assayer's office.

At the end of the main street, Savage found a livery which was little more than an oversized barn with a split-rail corral.

Once the horse was stabled, Savage asked the hostler about the hotel.

'What's it like?'

The wiry-looking man with thick, black hair said, 'Expensive.'

Savage nodded. 'Got a spare stall for me?'

'Nope,' the man grunted.

'Where's a good place to get somethin' to eat?'

'Café.'

'Where's that?'

'Main street.'

'Thanks,' Savage said.

'What for?'

'Nothin'.'

Savage left the man, a puzzled

expression on his face, as he walked from the livery, saddle bags over his left shoulder and the Yellow Boy rifle in his right hand. He ambled along the street drawing curious glances from some of the townsfolk.

As he passed one of the rough-built canvas covered saloon-tents, a drunk man staggered out. He stopped, gave Savage a disdainful look then spat on the ground. He was a bull of a man, with an unshaven face, and Savage could tell that the man was trouble.

The drunk screwed up his face and snorted. 'What the hell are you lookin' at?'

Savage walked around him and kept going. The drunk, however, wasn't finished just yet.

'The last time I saw a man wearin' a pair of britches like that he was lyin' dead on a battlefield near Five Forks.'

Savage stopped and turned to face the man.

Another man emerged from the saloon tent and placed a hand on the antagonist's arm.

'Leave it, Carter,' he cautioned him. 'The war's over.'

'So, what?' Carter snarled. 'I plan on killin' me another blue-belly.'

Savage dropped his gaze to the six-gun tucked in Carter's belt. His eyes came back up to meet Carter's challenging expression and he said, 'Listen to your friend, Carter. The war's over. It's been over for a long while.'

Shaking his head, Carter said, 'Nah, you ain't gettin' off that easy. I lost a lot of good friends to your lot. Time to get me some payback.'

Savage sighed and looked at Carter's friend. 'Are you in or out?'

The man frowned. 'What?'

'I want to know, if I have to kill stupid here, will I have to do the same to you?'

'Who the hell are you callin' stupid,' Carter snarled, and dove his right hand clumsily for his six-gun.

The rifle in Savage's right hand swung up, his thumb cocking the hammer. Once it was level, he squeezed the trigger. The impact of the .44 Henry slug at close range was brutal. It slammed into Carter's chest, meeting little resistance as it ripped its way through soft tissue.

In a cloud of crimson, it exploded out of his back, spraying the canvas of the tent behind him with droplets. Carter grunted as the air was forced from his body. He opened his mouth to speak but nothing came forth except a wet cough, which spattered flecks of blood on his lips.

Carter fell to the ground in an untidy heap. Jacking another round into the breech, Savage shifted his aim with the Winchester to point at the remaining man's face.

The man threw up his hands. 'Whoa, stranger. I ain't buyin' in.'

'Wise move,' Savage said. 'Tell the sheriff I'll be at the hotel.'

As Savage walked away, he could hear people start to spill out through the tent flap.

'What happened, Buck?' he heard one man ask.

'The stranger shot Carter.'

'Why would he do that?'

The answer was lost to Savage as he drew out of earshot.

* * *

Sheriff Charley Halley caught up with Savage at the hotel just as he was about to pay for his room.

'Mind if I have a word with you, stranger?' Halley asked. 'My name is Charley Halley. I'm what passes for law in Dead Man's Gulch.'

'Sure, ask away.'

'What's your name?'

'Jeff Savage.'

He waited for some sort of reaction but one wasn't forthcoming.

'How long do you plan on stayin', Savage?' the sheriff asked.

Looking down at the money he was about to pass across to the rotund desk clerk, Savage said, 'At these prices, one night. And that's only 'cause I couldn't get a stall at the livery.'

The last part of the comment was directed at the clerk, the Drifter making a point of letting him know he wasn't happy about parting with the five dollars he was being charged for the room.

He handed the money over and the clerk gave him a room key.

'You mind tellin' me your version of events with Carter?' Halley asked.

Savage shrugged. 'Not much to tell. He thought he could fight the war again and win. He was wrong.'

'At least there's one less of them now,' Halley muttered.

'Sorry?'

Halley realized he'd spoken aloud. He sighed. 'The feller you killed worked for Craig Vandal. He's the big man around this part of the mountains. Runs a big minin' operation about a mile from town. Carter was one of the mine guards. Vandal has around fifteen gunmen on his payroll to keep watch just in case the Chiricahuas decide to hit the mine. It wouldn't be the first time. They've even hit the Gulch a time or two.'

'I had me a run-in with them Apaches of yours,' Savage said, and went on to explain about his recent adventures.

Halley shook his head. 'Damn it. Did one of them fellers have a beard?'

'Yeah.'

'Yep, that was Charlie and Hank. They been workin' that creek for an age.'

'Not anymore they ain't,' said Savage.

Halley nodded. 'Do me a favor while you're here. Try not to get into any more trouble.'

'It ain't like I went lookin' for it, Sheriff,' Savage snapped.

Halley raised his hand. 'Just whoa up a mite. I know that, OK. All I'm askin' is for you to try and avoid any more.'

'I'll do my best. But if it comes knockin' at my door, I ain't goin' to run away.'

'Fair enough.'

'Where's a half-decent place in town for a man to get a feed,' Savage glanced at the clerk again, 'and it don't cost him the price of a good horse?'

The hint of an understanding smile touched Halley's lips. 'Try the Down and Out Saloon. It might cost you more than what you're used to payin' but the food won't kill you.'

'I'll try it out, thanks.'

* * *

For an emerging town, the office of Craig Vandal was quite lavish. Hand-tooled furniture had been shipped in, and ornate paneling adorned the walls. It was something that belonged back in St. Louis or Chicago, not in a tough mining town like Dead Man's Gulch.

Vandal was a solidly built man in his mid-fifties. His hair was gray and his face was lined from years of hard-work. As he stood up from behind his desk, the brown suit that he wore stretched taut and appeared to be at least one size too small on his frame.

'Who is this stranger anyway?' Vandal asked Curt Wedde.

Wedde was Vandal's right hand, bodyguard, and troubleshooter. He shrugged. 'I don't know. He drifted into town today.'

'Find out who he is,' Vandal ordered. 'If a stranger comes into my town and kills one of my men, I want to know who he is.'

'It weren't the stranger's fault, Craig,' Wedde told him. 'Carter pushed him into it from what I understand. He got drunk and decided the damn war wasn't finished. The stranger didn't want no part of it but Carter wouldn't let it drop. He could be like that.'

Vandal nodded in agreement. He'd seen Carter beat a man half to death for just looking at him. 'What about the other problem?'

'It'll be taken care of tonight,' Wedde told his boss.

'Make sure that it is. With Halley out

of the way, I can get my son out of that damned jail.'

'Are you sure you want it done this way? I mean, we could break him out of there,' Wedde suggested.

'Just do it like I said,' Vandal snapped.

'Sure, no problem.'

* * *

Savage had to agree with Halley. Sure, the meal had cost a little more than usual, but it was good. He guessed the meat was venison smothered in a thick gravy and was served with beans and potato.

It was early in the evening and night was an hour or so old. The saloon was busy with miners and other people from around the town. Although it was bustling, there was something not quite right about the atmosphere of the place. Savage supposed it could be his presence and the fact he'd killed one of their own, but thought it might be something else entirely.

He found out before he finished his meal.

While doing his rounds, Charley Halley entered the saloon and looked around. He spotted Savage and weaved his way through the tables of patrons until he reached him.

'How's the meal?'

'You were right, it's good.'

Savage noticed Halley looking about, not really taking notice of their conversation.

'Expectin' trouble?' Savage asked.

Halley's head snapped back at the mention of the word. 'What?'

'I asked if you were expectin' trouble?'

Halley frowned. 'No. At least I hope not. Have you heard somethin'?'

Savage forked a piece of gravy-soaked meat into his mouth.

'Nope,' he managed to get out while he chewed.

Once more, Halley looked about the room. Suddenly a scuffle broke out at the bar. Two large men grabbed each other and a couple of their friends latched onto them. Cursing, Halley walked toward them.

'Hey, knock it off you two,' he called above the noise.

A sixth sense told Savage that something about the scuffle was wrong and his suspicions were confirmed a few moments later. Placing his knife on the table, Savage dropped his right hand to where the Remington rested in its holster.

He eased it out so that the cocked six-gun lay on his lap ready to use at a moment's notice.

While Halley was helping break up the fight, two men moved in behind him and the hairs stood up on the back of Savage's neck. From a table to the right, another man stood and headed towards the group. As he closed in behind them, the Drifter saw a long, thin knife blade down at his side.

Savage knew what was about to happen but now had an additional problem: his line of sight was obscured by another drinker. Without hesitation, he launched from his chair and moved swiftly towards the group. He watched as the would-be killer's knife arm came back and was set to drive the blade deep into the sheriffs back. A blow that would never be delivered.

Using his left hand, Savage locked the man's collar in a vice-like grip and hauled him backward so that he staggered and went down hard on his butt. With his right hand, Savage wielded the Remington like a club, sending a crashing blow across the head of the man on the sheriff's right.

It made a sickening crunching sound and the man dropped where he'd stood. Then Savage brought it back in the opposite direction, just as the man on the left turned his head to see what was happening.

The Remington's barrel caught him across the bridge of his nose, shattering it in a spray of hot blood. As the stricken man fell to the floor, Savage turned back to face the would-be assassin with the knife. He looked up at the Drifter and started to come off the floor with a snarl of rage.

Without a second's hesitation, Savage raised the Remington and blew a hole in his skull. The knife wielder's head snapped back from the force of the slug and he flopped onto his back. Blood began to pool under his head and filter through the cracks in the floorboards.

Swinging back around, Savage brought the six-gun up and placed it against the head of the man nearest to him, which happened to be one of the men trying to break up the fight. The ratcheting sound of the gun hammer going back made him freeze.

Savage's voice grew cold. 'I suggest whatever it is you and your friends have planned, you might want to forget about it.'

Fear flashed through the man's eyes and the first words past his lips were, 'Don't shoot, Stranger!'

'Why not?' Savage asked. 'It would be about as much chance as you were goin' to give the sheriff.'

'What the hell, Savage?' alarm filled Halley's voice.

'These fellers had you lined up to kill,' Savage told him. 'The dead one on the floor was about to stick you with a knife.'

Halley looked at the corpse and saw the knife lying beside it. He switched his hot gaze to the others.

'Did Vandal put you up to this?' he snarled.

They remained silent.

'Well?'

Still nothing.

Halley shook his head. 'Get the hell out of my sight! Take your friends with you. Includin' the dead one.'

One of the men made a point of saying to Savage, 'You killed my friend. I'm goin' to kill you. You'd best be ready for it.'

'Get gone, French,' Halley snapped.

They watched them leave.

'You don't want to lock them up?' Savage asked.

'No, I got me enough troubles without addin' to them.'

'So, it would seem,' Savage allowed. 'If you don't mind, I'll go back to my meal?'

'Before you go, thanks.'

Savage looked him in the eyes and nodded. 'Watch your back, Halley.'

He went back to the remnants of his meal under the watchful gaze of the townsfolk. Once he was finished, Savage ordered a beer and relaxed while he drank it.

About thirty minutes after the shooting, Savage noticed a serious looking man enter the saloon. He was approximately thirty, had black hair and was maybe six-feet tall. He looked around the room then walked to the bar where he leaned across and spoke to the barkeep.

The barkeep pointed in Savage's direction and the man began to walk towards his table. As he came on,

Savage noticed the two six-guns. One sat in a holster against his right thigh, while the other was high-up on the left hip, but forward and positioned for a cross-draw.

Underneath the table, Savage freed his Remington once more. It sure was a town that kept a man on his toes.

The man sat down across from Savage and looked him over with a steady gaze before saying, 'You're causin' us some troubles, Stranger.'

'How do you figure that?' Savage asked him.

'You've been in town but five minutes and you've killed two men and banged up another two.'

'What's your point?'

'Maybe you should stay out of things that don't concern you,' the man warned.

'Maybe you should tell me your name,' Savage suggested. 'I like to know who's givin' me orders.'

'I'm Curt Wedde,' the man said. 'I work for Craig Vandal. Who are you?'

'Jeff Savage.'

Wedde nodded and waited expectantly for Savage to speak.

'Is there somethin' else?' Savage asked.

'Nope, I said what I wanted to say.'

'Well I'll have my say then,' Savage told him. 'First, I don't take kindly to fellers tryin' to kill me. It has the tendency to rile me some, as you are aware. Second, I won't stand by and see men commit murder. And third, I've decided to stay a while. Take that back to your boss and tell him to shove it.'

Wedde gave him a thin smile and nodded. 'I'll do that. But don't say you weren't warned.'

Savage watched him stand and leave. He became aware of the prying eyes of bystanders and when he looked at them, he saw apprehension on their faces. There was obviously something seriously wrong in Dead Man's Gulch. But what?

* * *

'If he gets in the way again, kill him,' Craig Vandal said to Wedde. There was a granite-like edge to the mine boss' voice that had become more prominent since his son's incarceration at the jail.

'There's somethin' about him, boss, that don't sit right,' Wedde said, voicing his concern.

'Like what?' Vandal snapped.

'I don't know. I looked into his eyes and there's nothin' there. They're like bottomless pits.'

'You're seeing things that aren't there,' Vandal snorted, dismissing his man's instincts. 'He's just a nosy drifter who'll get the damn thing cut off if he isn't careful about where he sticks it.'

Wedde shrugged, an uncertain expression on his face.

'Anyway,' Vandal continued, 'we've got two days until the trial. And my son isn't going to hang, so we need to come up with another way of getting him out, fast.'

3

Savage let out a shuddering moan and rolled off the whore he knew as Sylvie, exposing her lithe body to the moonlight that filtered through the window in the small room above the saloon. It reflected off her sweat-streaked form, her large breasts luminescent.

'Damn, cowboy,' Sylvie panted. 'I ain't been rode like that in a long time. I might have to give you one for free. If you want another that is?'

Savage sat up and swung his legs over the side of the bed, unsure whether the anger he felt was because he'd betrayed his late wife's memory, or because he'd paid five dollars for a room that he wasn't likely to use.

'We'll see.'

Sylvie sat up and worked her way across the bed. She then sat with a leg either side of Savage and leaned in close so that her breasts flattened against his back. She ran her long fingers gently across the nape of his neck sending a shiver down his spine.

She whispered in his ear, 'How's that?'

'OK, I guess.'

Her hands started to move down his arms in a gentle stroking motion. Then further until they reached his hips. Then Sylvie started to move her hands around the front.

Savage was about to stop her when the bedroom door burst open and slammed back against the wall.

'I told you I'd kill you, you son of a bitch!' a voice filled the room.

Savage dived forward off the side of the bed and onto the floor just as the cut-down shotgun in French's hands roared deafeningly.

Sylvie's scream was cut short as the charge ripped her flesh apart and she fell in a bloody heap across Savage's back, painting him red.

He rolled her aside and came up off

the floor with a bellow of rage. Startled at the sight of the naked, bloodied figure before him, French fumbled as he tried to reload. He snapped the breech closed after inserting one cartridge and was struggling to bring it up when Savage was upon him.

He ripped the shotgun from French's grasp and brought the butt up in a sweeping blow that caught French under the chin. The man's head snapped back and he fell against the wall, stunned. A blinding rage consumed Savage. He rammed the barrels of the shotgun viciously into French's mouth, splitting lips and shattering teeth. Then, without thought or hesitation, he pulled the trigger.

* * *

Halley blanched as he looked once more at French and shook his head. He turned back towards Savage who sat on the bed dressed only in his pants. The blood on his body was now dried crusts on his skin.

'How much longer is that damned undertaker goin' to be?' Savage asked, impatiently.

Halley shrugged. 'I knew there was goin' to be trouble with that son of a bitch.'

'Well, why in hell didn't you lock him up?' Savage barked angrily.

'Yes, I should've! All right? I can't change it now.'

But Savage wasn't finished. 'What's wrong with this town, anyway? Since I been here I've run into nothin' but trouble.'

'Bobby Vandal,' Halley stated.

'What?'

'The problem is Bobby Vandal,' Halley told him. 'Ever since I locked him up, this town has gone plumb crazy.'

'Well let him out,' Savage suggested.

'I can't.'

'Why not?'

''Cause he's goin' to hang for

murder,' Halley told Savage. 'That was why they tried to kill me. Because I got Craig Vandal's son locked up and by God, I aim to see that son of a bitch swing.'

'Don't you have yourself a deputy?'

'Nope. It's just me.'

There was a commotion outside in the hall and Craig Vandal filled the doorway. His eyes settled on Savage and his face became hard.

'Are you Savage?'

'What if I am?'

'Ever since you arrived in this town, all you've done is interfere with things that don't concern you,' Vandal snarled.

'Who are you?'

'I'm Craig Vandal, and I want you the hell out of my town.'

Savage stood up, his muscular chest rippled with the movement. He walked across the room and stopped short of the red-faced man.

'I tell you what, *Mr.* Vandal. You tell your men to stop tryin' to kill me and I'll stop shootin' them.'

'I'll tell *you* what, I'll do you one better. How about you drag your drifting ass out of my town and everyone will be happy.'

'Don't push me, Vandal,' Savage hissed. 'You've seen what can happen when people do.'

'I'll give you until noon tomorrow,' Vandal said, undeterred. 'After that, don't expect to leave.'

Vandal spun on his heel and stormed from the room.

'Really showed concern for his man, didn't he?' Savage commented.

'He ain't worried about his men, or the fact that you're killin' them,' Halley said. 'He's worried about you. No one has ever stood up to him or his men like that before. He's worried that if you become tangled in this, then he won't be able to get his boy out of jail before he hangs. You saw how desperate he's become when he had his men try and kill me. I might not be so lucky next time.'

'Halley, you said before you didn't

have yourself a deputy. You do now. I'll sign on until after the trial and Vandal's son swings rope.'

'I couldn't ask you to do that, Savage,' Halley told him. 'Besides, for there to be an unbiased trial, he'll need to be shifted to Albuquerque. I talked about it with Judge McArdle today and he agreed.'

'Well, shift him then. I'll help you. Hell, I'm headed there anyway,' Savage said.

'Are you sure?'

Savage nodded.

'OK. Come by the jail in the morning and I'll swear you in. In the meantime, get yourself a bath and wash all that blood off you.'

'No, we do it tonight. Before dawn anyway.'

'Why so soon?'

'Vandal strikes me as an impatient man,' Savage surmised. 'I think we should move his kid sooner rather than later. Before they get wind of our plans, otherwise they'll try to ambush us on the road and break him free.'

Halley nodded. 'All right, we'll do it that way.'

'I'll get cleaned up and meet you at the jail. We'll need horses.'

Halley told him where he could acquire some and a few other things as well.

'I'll see you in a couple of hours. That'll give us a good head start before daylight.'

Halley nodded. 'Until then.'

* * *

They escorted Bobby Vandal out the back door to put him on the back of a bay horse that Savage had got from the hostler. The night was cool and mostly clear. The stars above glittered like small flashing lights around the large moon. Every so often a cloud scudded across it, casting a fleeting shadow over the mountains.

'You won't get away with this,' Bobby said loudly.

'Shut up,' Halley snapped at him.

'Why?' he shouted this time. 'Are you afraid someone will hear!'

He opened his mouth to continue, but a bunched fist from Savage smashed into it, chopping his words off abruptly. He buckled at the knees and Savage caught him by the arm.

'You were told to shut up, now get on that horse.'

Once Bobby was on the bay, Halley and the Drifter climbed into their saddles. They turned their horses and commenced the ride out of town.

On the outskirts, Savage asked, 'How long do you figure before they know we're gone?'

'I'll give it half a day,' Halley allowed. 'If we're lucky.'

'Let's hope we are,' Savage said.

For the few hours until dawn, the going was slow. The narrow trail twisted and turned through the tall timber and rocky terrain. The last thing they needed was for one of the horses to pull up lame.

Dawn found them ten miles from Dead Man's Gulch and with a good head start. Or so they thought. Someone had witnessed their hasty exit and now, only five miles behind them, was a group of men led by Curt Wedde.

* * *

'We'll stop here for the night,' Halley told Savage. 'The horses need the rest.'

'Sure, why not. I'll get a fire goin' while you take care of our guest.'

'Do you think they're still back there?'

Savage had checked their backtrail earlier and seen the riders topping the next ridge over from the one they'd been on at the time.

'They'll still be comin' on,' Savage said. 'Tomorrow I'll see if I can throw a false trail for them to follow.'

Bobby Vandal snorted derisively. 'They'll catch up, and when they do, you're both dead.'

'You won't have cause to worry,' Savage said. 'I aim to shoot you before I die.'

'If you like, once we've done what needs doin', I'll take first watch,' Savage offered to Halley.

'Sure, if you want. It's up to you. I suggest we do it two hours about so we get a few short shifts and can get some frequent sleep.'

Savage nodded. 'Sounds good to me.'

Sometime after midnight, he wouldn't be so sure.

* * *

The sound of a gun hammer going back snapped Savage from his slumber. His eyes flickered open and recognized the six-gun in the hand of the man who stood over him.

'I'm guessin' that you've been woke up in better ways than the one that's happenin' now,' Wedde said to him.

'I take it that this ain't a social visit?' Savage asked.

'Ain't that the truth. Get on your feet.'

Slowly Savage got to his feet and stood rock still while he waited to see what was going to happen next.

Halley appeared from out of the dark escorted by two men. He looked at the Drifter and said, 'I'm sorry, I don't know what happened.'

'You went to sleep is what happened,' one of the men guffawed.

'Cut me loose, Curt,' Bobby called out. 'I got some business to finish with these two.'

Savage cursed Halley inwardly. It was a mistake that would, he was certain, cost them their lives. Standing there, he was aware that no one had moved to take his Remington from the holster around his waist. He might still have a chance, albeit a slim one.

It was Bobby Vandal who swung the odds in Savage's favor.

As soon as he was freed, he strode purposefully across to where Halley stood, under the guard of one of the men's gun. Bobby snatched the six-gun from his grasp and shot Halley in the stomach.

The sound of the shot took everyone by surprise, but Savage recovered the quickest. He drew the Remington with blinding speed and opened fire on the group. There were six men in total who'd crept up on them and after Savage had fired two shots, they were down to four plus Bobby.

By the time they recovered, Savage had disappeared into the dark.

'Where did he go?' he heard Bobby Vandal scream before a flurry of wild gunshots pierced the darkness.

He heard Wedde say, 'Stop that damned shootin', you ain't goin' to hit nothin'. Get out there and find him.'

Carefully, Savage circled about the camp until he found their horses. He unhooked the reins from around a tree limb then slapped them hard on their muscular rumps. The startled beasts took off into the darkness.

'The horses! He's after the horses!'

the shout filled the night.

Savage found cover behind some rocks and listened as Vandal's men scattered into the surrounding gloom after their mounts. He waited for five minutes before he figured that it was quiet enough to sneak back into camp and get his saddle and rifle.

He checked on Halley but it was clear the sheriff was dead. He then hurried past the low burning campfire, over to where his saddle and rifle lay. He picked them up and turned in time to see Curt Wedde enter the dim firelight.

'I figured you wouldn't go far without your horse,' he gloated.

'You figured right,' Savage allowed. 'What now?'

Wedde shrugged. 'Now I shoot you.'

'Figured as much,' Savage said and made one more desperate move. He dropped his saddle onto the fire.

An unexpected flurry of embers billowed up and caught Wedde by surprise. He jerked the trigger but the bullet flew wide enough of its intended target to be of no danger.

The Yellow Boy in Savage's hands whiplashed and the slug dealt Wedde a devastating blow to the chest, knocking him backward onto the ground. The echoes of the gunshots seemed to roll forever through the night and the Drifter knew that he would have company soon enough.

He didn't bother to check on Wedde, instead pulled his smoldering saddle from the fire and hurried to his horse. Once it was saddled, he retrieved his saddlebags with the supplies and extra ammunition. As he walked back past Wedde, the supposedly dead man coughed. It was a wet, gurgling sound that indicated that his lungs were filling with blood.

Savage paused. 'If you live long enough, tell Bobby I'm goin' to come for him. Tell him there's a new law in town. My law.'

Wedde opened his mouth to speak but died before anything could emerge.

'Never mind,' Savage said, 'I'll tell him myself.'

4

Craig Vandal was good and mad. Not about the men he'd lost. They could be replaced, including Wedde. No, he was mad because Savage had escaped.

'How is it that you all let one man best you?' he roared. 'Am I surrounded by total incompetence?'

His loud voice filled the lamp-lit office and filtered outside onto the boardwalk where the others awaited further orders. They'd arrived back in Dead Man's Gulch late in the afternoon and now, as Craig Vandal berated his son, another sun was sinking behind the pine-clad mountains.

'It was dark, Pa,' Bobby Vandal protested. 'Besides, I got Halley for you.'

'*I got Halley for you!*' Vandal mimicked his son. 'You dumb son of a bitch, Halley wasn't the dangerous one.

Now, Savage is out there somewhere and we don't know where.'

Suddenly the door crashed open and a man burst in, a look of excitement on his face.

'He's here!'

'What?' Craig Vandal snapped.

'He's here, he just rode into town.'

'Stop talking in riddles man and spit it out,' Craig Vandal said impatiently. 'Who's here?'

'Savage just rode in, leadin' the sheriff's horse. He was draped over it and all.'

'He must've went back for the body after we cleared out,' said Bobby Vandal.

'And now he's here,' Craig Vandal snarled. 'I want that son of a bitch gone.'

'I'll see to it.'

'No. You stay out of the way,' Craig Vandal snapped. His gaze settled on the man who'd brought the news. 'Tell Finch he's in charge and to get rid of Savage. I don't care how.'

The man hesitated.

'What?' his boss snapped.

'Are you sure you want to kill another lawman?'

'The only law around here is me. Now go.'

When the man had left, Craig Vandal's harsh gaze returned to his son. 'I want you out of town until all this blows over. Head on over to Bad Tooth and lay low.'

'But that place is full of murderers and cutthroats,' Bobby protested.

'Then you should fit right in, shouldn't you?' the older Vandal sneered. 'Don't you go trying to buck me, boy. You'll go there, and there you'll stay until I say otherwise. It isn't like you've not been there before.'

Bobby was about to continue the argument but a withering look from his father changed his mind. Instead, he turned about and left the room.

Craig Vandal watched him go and wondered, for the first time, whether he'd bitten off more than he could chew.

* * *

Savage's first job was to deliver Halley's body to the undertaker's. The next was to go to the jail and prepare for the visitors he was bound to have. He loaded all the guns in the gun rack, and moved the pinto out back, leaving it saddled. He then made himself some coffee on the small potbellied stove.

Unexpectedly, it wasn't Craig Vandal's men who paid him the first visit. It was Judge Perry McArdle. He was a large man with gray hair and beard. His face was lined and his frown gave him a perpetual worried expression.

'I won't keep you but a moment, Mr. Savage,' McArdle said. 'Sheriff Halley told me about you and your offer to help before you left town with Bobby Vandal. I know that the sheriff is dead. Would you mind telling me what happened?'

Savage filled him in on the events leading up to his return to Dead Man's Gulch.

'It's a bad business when a man can get away with murder, Mr. Savage,' McArdle said grimly. 'What are your plans now that — well you know?'

The Drifter peeled back the left side of his jacket to reveal the deputy sheriff's badge pinned to his shirt. 'Halley gave me this and swore me in. As far as I'm concerned it still counts. If you've no objections, I'd like to continue the duties accordingly?'

McArdle nodded. 'I can only think of one. Maybe you should pin the sheriff's badge on instead.'

'OK. Be aware, however, that you might find some of my methods unconventional.'

'I don't care what you have to do, Mr. Savage,' McArdle responded. 'You do whatever it takes to bring the sheriff's murderer to justice and rid this town of Craig Vandal. Do you need help? Can I find you a deputy?'

Savage shook his head. 'I'll deal with it all on my own.'

'Then I can only wish you luck, Mr.

Savage because Craig Vandal worships his son and won't stop until either of you is dead.'

'Savage!' a voice shouted from outside. 'Come on out, Savage, or we're comin' in after you.'

'It sounds like things are about to start, Judge,' Savage said as he walked to the window and peered out through a crack in the curtain. 'I suggest you go out the back way so they don't see you.'

'What do you plan on doing?' McArdle asked.

'My job,' Savage said stonily. 'Now get outta here.'

'Savage!' the voice shouted again.

'Go, Judge, I'm about to be busy.'

McArdle slipped out the back door while Savage picked up a cut-down shotgun from the pile of guns on the scarred desktop. He walked across to the door and opened it. Once out on the boardwalk, he was confronted by ten armed men.

'What do you want?' he asked the man at the head of the group.

'Mr. Vandal wants you run outta Dead Man's Gulch,' he said. 'He put me in charge of doin' it.'

'And what if I ain't goin' to run?'

'Then you'll be buried here.'

'Just so you know, I'm the new town sheriff.'

There was a moment of hesitation before the speaker said, 'So what?'

'Before anythin' happens, I want to understand. If I refuse to leave town, you all intend to kill me. Is that right?'

'Got it in one,' the man sneered.

'OK then,' Savage said and brought the shotgun into firing position.

In the gloom of the surrounding twilight, the orange flame that spewed forth from the twin barrels was amazingly bright. The sound of the shot rolled loudly along the vacant street as the man was thrust violently backward, his chest ripped to shreds by the buckshot.

The other men scattered, then started to fire back once they'd regained their composure. But by then,

Savage was back inside the jail and the door was closed.

Slugs hammered out a staccato sound as they peppered the thin plank walls of the jail. Some smashed through, filling the interior with wicked splinters as well as flying lead.

Savage took cover near the window with another cut-down shotgun. He used the twin barrels to break the glass then poked them through.

He squeezed both triggers and the weapon roared, releasing both deadly payloads at once. A howl of pain could be heard outside as one of the shooters stopped lead balls.

Savage dropped the gun to the floor and took the Yellow Boy from the desktop. He poked its octagonal barrel out the window and started levering and firing methodically at any targets that presented themselves.

A volley of gunfire from outside smashed into the remaining glass sending razor-sharp shards flying across the room. Savage ducked back when he felt the sting of cutting glass on his cheek.

He wiped at the burning spot and his hand came away streaked with red.

'Son of a bitch,' he muttered and let loose with his own flurry of shots and was rewarded with another yelp of pain.

Savage knew he couldn't stay there. The safest place for him was outside of town somewhere. He needed to hide until he could formulate some sort of plan that would effectively bring the Vandals down. If he stayed here, they might get lucky and kill him. Out there in the wilderness was a whole other story.

On his way to the back door, he collected one of the cut-down shotguns and a box of shells. Once outside, Savage climbed onto the pinto's back and put him into a steady lope towards the outskirts of town and relative safety.

When Craig Vandal's men realized that the shooting from within the jail had stopped, it was too late. They burst in through the door and discovered an empty room. Their boss was not going to be happy at all.

* * *

'Finch didn't stand a chance, boss,' the man called Howard said. 'He just cut loose with that cannon of his before we knew what was happenin'. On top of that, we got two other men wounded as well.'

All of Craig Vandal's patience was gone. It had been driven away and replaced by a burning rage that threatened to consume all rational thought inside of his mind.

He stormed across the room and back again. After several minutes of silence and much thought, he managed to calm himself again before he spoke. 'Organize some men and get searching for him. Find him and kill him. I'll give two thousand dollars to the man who does it.'

The man's eyes bulged, his mouth agape. 'We'll get right on it.'

'And try not to get killed. At the rate I'm losing men, there'll be none left pretty soon.'

Craig Vandal watched him go. His mind, however, was elsewhere. His men weren't up for the job of dealing with Savage. The $2,000 reward might spur them on for a while but when it came down to it, Savage was more than a match for them. What he needed was someone as ruthless as the man they were hunting. And he knew just where to find him.

* * *

When the telegram arrived in Cobalt Creek the following morning, the manhunter known as Rawhide Allen was trying to decide whether to kill a man. Not that the man needed killing, nor was it a job. Rawhide Allen wanted to kill the man just because he could.

'Mr. Allen,' the telegrapher said warily. 'I have a message for you.'

Allen broke his train of thought to stare at the timid looking man. Allen's cold blue eyes sent a chill down the man's spine. The telegrapher's hand trembled as he held out the piece of paper.

The manhunter dropped his fork onto his plate of half-eaten bacon and eggs and snatched the telegram from the man's grasp.

The telegrapher jumped involuntarily and turned quickly; almost running from the café.

While reading the message, Allen resumed his breakfast and shoveled a forkful of food into his mouth. He started chewing but stopped when he reached the part about being paid $2,000 to kill a man.

He liked getting paid but the killing part was the best. He'd learned his craft well in the war between the states when he'd ridden with the border raiders of one William Quantrill.

Pushing the remainder of his meal away, Allen stuffed the telegram into his top-right pocket and stood erect. He was lean and tall at a shade under 6-foot-4. He smoothed his dark trousers and adjusted the holstered Remington he wore on his hips. Distractedly, he raised his hand and scratched at the dark stubble on his square jaw then ran it through his almost black hair and picked up his battered, dark low-crowned hat.

Remembering that he needed to pay for his meal, Allen placed his hat back on the table and reached into his hip pocket and took out his folding money. He peeled off a five-dollar note and threw it on the table, retrieved his hat and hurried for the door. He had a hundred and fifty miles to ride for the chance to kill a man.

As he stepped out onto the boardwalk, he saw the rat-faced storekeeper who'd looked down his nose at Allen when he'd gone for supplies. The same man who'd judged him on his appearance. Little did the storekeeper know how lucky he was.

* * *

For two days, the hunt for Savage continued throughout the hills and ridges surrounding Dead Man's Gulch. A cold campfire they happened upon was the closest they'd come to finding him.

Things, however, were about to change. On the morning of the third day, above them on a rocky ridge, Savage sighted along the barrel of the Yellow Boy, the foresight settled on the lead rider.

Off in the trees to his left, he heard a bird call. The sound stayed his finger on the trigger before he took up the slack. A move that might well have saved his life.

The call was answered by another further along the ridge and a little down slope.

Savage drew the rifle barrel back, listened then squatted down behind the rocks where he was hidden.

Over the course of the next minute,

there were no more sounds. He could only assume that the Chiricahua were closing in on the unsuspecting riders below. So be it. They were here to kill him. If the Apaches could help his cause, then all the better.

Savage didn't have to wait long. A yell signaled the onset of the attack and the surrounding ridges erupted with the sound of gunfire.

As Savage looked on, he saw Apaches emerge from the trees. There were ten more of them than he'd figured on. They hit the searchers from the flank and in the blink of an eye, they were amongst them.

The gunshots died away as the fighting became hand-to-hand. Savage saw a rider go down with a Chiricahua brave on top of him. A knife glittered as it rose and fell three times. An Apache fell from his horse, clubbed about the head with a six-gun. More flailing bodies fell from horses as the fighting intensified.

A blood-curdling cry echoed around

the hills, as a wounded man had the hair ripped from his head, audible above the din of battle. An Indian stiffened when his own knife was driven into his throat, sending a cascade of bright-red blood down his naked torso.

Suddenly two men on horseback broke away from the group, riding furiously away from the scene of carnage. Savage watched them go, the surviving Apaches hot on their tail.

He waited for ten or so minutes to see if they would return and when there was no sign, he led his horse down off the ridge to check for survivors. To his astonishment, he found one.

Savage left the pinto ground-hitched a dozen yards from the macabre scene and walked amongst the bodies, cradling the Yellow Boy. Cocked and ready to fire.

The coppery smell of fresh blood was so powerful, the salty taste was on his palette and he spat on the ground to remove it. He walked slowly between the bodies until he came across the man whose scalping he'd witnessed. He paused and looked down at him. The face was streaked with red lines and a bead of sweat ran —

'Son of a bitch, you're alive.'

The dead man was indeed alive and when Savage spoke, it was enough to start the man's body trembling. His eyes snapped open, a deep-seated pain obvious to see.

'You — you gotta help me,' he pleaded.

'Why?'

'You can't . . . ' he swallowed hard. 'You can't leave me here for them Apaches.'

'Why?'

'I — I know where to find Bobby Vandal.'

That got Savage's attention. 'Where is he?'

'Get me on a horse.'

'Tell me where.'

'C'mon Savage, them Cherrycows could be here at any time,' the man pleaded.

'Then talk fast.'

There was a pregnant pause as a wave of pain washed over the disfigured man, then he said, 'His old man sent him to Bad Tooth.'

'Where's that?'

'Damn it, Savage,' the man cursed through gritted teeth.

'Where!'

'Northeast of here, about a day and a half ride. It's a bad place, a whole lotta outlaws hole up there. All right?'

'Sure.'

'Now, what about the horse? You'll have to help me, I can't seem to move.'

Savage let his eyes drift over the man's body. The gaping gash in the man's middle might have something to do with that. Some of the bloodstained coils of intestine had spilled like snakes onto the coarse grass beside the dying man.

Savage nodded grimly. 'Sure, I'll help you.'

The man smiled hopefully. 'Thanks . . . '

The sound of the shot whiplashed

and the man's head snapped to the side, the grass beside it sprayed with flecks of blood. The Drifter stood motionless, staring down at the corpse.

'You're welcome.'

5

By the time, Rawhide Allen reached Dead Man's Gulch, he was mean. Killing mean, and the throbbing pain emanating from his ass wasn't making his mood any better. The boil had come up the previous day, beginning as an angry red dot that continued to grow until it was a hard red mass the size of a double-eagle.

Which did not bode well for anyone who crossed him and the first person to bear the brunt of his foul temper was the hostler.

'What can I do for you, stranger?' he asked Allen, who led his horse in through the door.

'Need a stall,' Allen grunted.

The hostler shook his head. 'Sorry, they're all full. I can put him in the corral out the back if you like. Horse'll still be looked after the same as the rest.'

'Stall.'

Again, the hostler shook his head. 'I already told you. They're full up.'

Allen let go of the horse's reins and moved forward, closing the gap between them in the blink of an eye, startling the man before him. The killer drew his six-gun and lashed out with it. There was a sickening crack as the barrel smashed into the side of the hostler's head.

The man dropped like a stone but Allen wasn't done yet. He gritted his teeth, leaned down and hit the man twice more. When he was finished, blood flowed freely from the lacerations to the man's head and face.

Allen gave him a solid kick to the ribs for good measure and the hostler moaned.

'When you're ready, put the damned horse in a stall,' the killer hissed. 'Or next time I'll kill you.'

Allen left the livery and walked along the street until he found Vandal's office. He pushed his way through the door and inside found Craig Vandal in the middle of berating another man.

'What the hell is going on around here? All you men seem to do is get killed. If it isn't that son of a bitch Savage, it's the damned Apaches. What does it take to get rid of one damned man?'

'Well now, I believe that would be me.'

The two men looked at Allen.

'Who are you?' Vandal snapped.

'I'm Rawhide Allen. The feller you sent for.'

'Finally. About damned time we had someone that could be relied upon to get the job done. I'm Craig Vandal,' Vandal said, seemingly relieved. He returned his gaze to the surviving member of the search party and snarled, 'Get the hell out of here.'

When the door closed, Allen said, 'Before we get to talkin' business, we need to discuss somethin' else.'

'And what might that be?' Craig Vandal asked impatiently.

'The two thousand dollars you have on offer.'

'What about it?'

'It ain't enough.'

'What?' Vandal snapped.

'I want five thousand,' Allen stated.

'You what?' Vandal spluttered, his eyes bulging in surprise.

'From what I can gather since walkin' in here, there's Apaches involved. That alone sends the price up. Also, the fact that you've been losin' men that have been sent after him, tells me this is goin' to be no ordinary manhunt. So, I will require more money.'

Vandal wasn't used to being dictated to and was certainly not happy about it and made his displeasure clear. 'I'm not paying you that much, damn it. I don't care what your reputation is. No man is worth that much.'

With the gnawing pain in his ass burrowing into the deep recesses of his brain, Allen briefly considered shooting the man before him in the head and leaving. Instead, he turned around and headed towards the door.

'Wait!'

Allen paused, a thin smile on his lips. He turned back to face Vandal.

'OK, five thousand.'

Allen nodded. 'I get two thousand up front, whether I kill him or not.'

Once more a resentful look flashed across Vandal's face. 'Fine.'

Vandal turned away from Allen and went to a safe that stood against the far wall. He unlocked it and riffled through a bundle of notes until he had the required amount. He closed and locked the safe again before turning back to Allen. He passed it over. 'There.'

Allen stuffed the money into his coat pocket.

'If you find the man who just left, he'll tell you what you need to know about Savage's last known whereabouts.'

Allen nodded. 'Where can I find a doctor?'

'What? Never mind,' Vandal said, shaking his head. 'Four down on the other side of the street. What do you want with the doctor, anyway? You seem fine.'

'I'm like you, Vandal. I have a great big pain in my ass.'

* * *

Naiche was in trouble and was convinced that he was about to die at the hands of the white-eyes who'd found him riding on his own. He was scared. He should have listened to Taza and not wandered off. But how was he to know what would happen? This was Chiricahua land. His father's land. The whites did not belong here, not that they hadn't ventured this far before.

But here they were. The three men had surprised him as he'd ridden along a trail beside a dry, rocky creek bed that ran between two small, rock-strewn ridges sparsely dotted with pines.

He struggled against the grip of one of his captors. He was strong for his age, almost twelve summers, but the tall man with the straggly beard was stronger. He and his two friends, Long Hair and Big Nose were unevenly matched against the youth.

'Hold the little bastard still will you so I can cut him with my knife,' Long Hair growled in a deep voice. 'You get hold of the little bastard too, Rhett.'

The man with the big nose moved in on the opposite side to Straggly Beard and grabbed Naiche's free arm in a firm grip.

'I got the little sumbitch, Jimmy,' Rhett snickered. 'Scalp him first, before you go and kill him.'

Naiche snarled and wrenched his arm free from Straggly Beard.

'Damn it, Sheb,' Jimmy cursed, 'keep hold of him.'

'Come here you,' Sheb snarled and grabbed a fistful of Naiche's hair to keep him still.

Jimmy moved in closer to the struggling Naiche and as he brought up the knife he declared with a smile, 'This is goin' to hurt you more than me Injun.'

Naiche's struggles intensified when he felt the stinging burn as the tip of the razor-sharp blade pierce the skin just below his hairline. He gasped and tried to bite back the cry of pain that threatened to burst from his lips. He was determined not to give them the satisfaction; even when the blade moved, slicing his scalp open to the bone. Blood started to run freely from the already gaping wound.

'That's it, Jimmy, cut the little sumbitch,' Rhett said gleefully. 'Cut him good.'

Naiche tried to pull his head away but they held him firmly in place. The burning pain spread with the journey of the knife. Two inches now.

The pain was becoming unbearable and tears flowed from the Apache boy's eyes and mixed with the blood.

Suddenly a voice said, 'Let the boy go and you three maggot eatin' scum might live through what's left of the day.'

Heads turned and four sets of eyes locked onto the man on the pinto with a rifle pointed in their general direction.

Jimmy took a step back from his grizzly task and stared angrily at the stranger. He said, 'Mister, this ain't got nothin' to do with you so I suggest you ride on.'

'Yeah, that's it,' Rhett cackled, 'ride the hell on afore we kill you too.'

Savage saw the knife in Jimmy's hand, noticed the bloody blade. He diverted his gaze and saw the blood-streaked face of the boy.

'Bastards,' he muttered before his look grew icy and turned back to Jimmy.

'What is it you're doin' to the kid?'

'I'm goin' to scalp him,' Jimmy said, his voice conveying a challenging tone. 'I was just startin' when you showed up. Now get gone.'

Without hesitation, Savage shot Jimmy with the Yellow Boy. The .44

Henry slug hit him hard in the chest and blew a fist-sized hole when it exited his back. Blood blossomed bright on Jimmy's chest and his mouth dropped open in shock. He took a couple of steps back and sat down hard on the ground.

The clack-clack of the lever signaled another round being chambered. The Yellow Boy whiplashed again and this shot blew Jimmy's head apart. He fell back onto the grass and lay still.

'You bastard! You murderin' son of a bitch!' Rhett shouted, his euphoria shattered at the sight of his friend's violent death.

'Let the kid go,' Savage ordered as he jacked a third round into the rifle's breech.

'But he's a stinkin' Apache brat!' Rhett shouted again. 'He ain't nothin' to you, you, sumbitch.'

'Got that right. But at least I'm alive.'

'Huh?'

A heartbeat later, Rhett was dead on the ground, a bloodied hole in his head, eyes staring sightlessly up at the cloudless sky. The sound of the shot echoed throughout the mountains.

Savage worked the lever again and shifted his aim. 'How about you? Are you tired of livin'?'

Sheb pulled his hand from Naiche's arm, as though it was made of lava. He threw his arms up in the air and cried out, 'Don't shoot! I don't want to die. Not for no Apache kid.'

'Get out of here before you wind up like your friends,' Savage ordered him. 'If I see you around again, I'm just as likely to kill you too.'

Sheb made out the edge of the sheriff's star protruding from the cover of Savage's buckskin coat.

'You're a lawman,' he blurted out. 'You shot them down cold. You ain't supposed to do that, you're the law.'

Savage raised the rifle and aimed it at Sheb's heart. With a look of unbridled fear on his face, Sheb turned and fled towards the nearby horses. In a single bound he was in the saddle and spurring away as fast as the mount could carry him.

'Are you OK, boy?' Savage asked Naiche.

The young Apache just looked at Savage, not speaking.

Savage switched to Spanish. 'Are you OK, boy?'

Naiche nodded. 'Yes.'

Savage climbed down from the pinto. 'Let's get that head of yours cleaned up so we can see what we're dealin' with.'

Naiche backed away, an alarmed expression on his face.

'Take it easy, boy, I only want to have a look at that head of yours,' Savage tried to soothe his anxiety. 'What's your name?'

'Naiche,' he said, eyeing the white man warily.

'All right,' Savage said, taking his canteen from his saddle. 'What are you doin' out here on your lonesome?'

'Riding,' Naiche grunted.

Savage bent down and ripped the sleeves from one of the dead men's shirt and soaked one in water. He stepped toward the boy and said calmly, 'Not the best of places to be ridin' on your own.'

'I am not alone,' Naiche said. 'I am with my brother and some of my people.'

Trying not to show concern, Savage started to wipe away the blood. 'That's a nasty lookin' cut you got there. I'll wrap it up for you and you can get your brother to take care of it.'

The defiant look on Naiche's face fell away. 'Taza will not be happy.'

The hand with the rag in it froze as realization dawned on Savage. 'Did you say your brother's name is Taza?'

'Yes,' said Naiche.

'Oh hell,' Savage muttered.

'*Qué es?*' Naiche asked. 'What is it?'

'I just realized who your father is, boy,' Savage told him.

A look of pride came to Naiche's face and he straightened noticeably. 'Yes, my father is Cochise.'

6

Savage tied off the rag around Naiche's head and asked, 'Where is your father, boy?'

'He is off with his warriors killing white-eyes,' Naiche told him.

It wasn't long back that Cochise and Savage had crossed paths in Arizona territory. Although that had ended well, he wasn't sure that this time would have the same outcome.

Nodding, Savage asked, 'Then, where is your brother?'

Naiche pointed over Savage's shoulder. 'He is there.'

A sinking feeling settled in the pit of Savage's stomach. He turned and looked at one of the small ridges. Sitting there amongst the sparse scatterings of pines, were six mounted Chiricahua Apaches, no more than a hundred yards away.

Stepping back from Naiche, Savage leaned down and picked up the Yellow Boy, making sure there was a live round under the hammer. He also made sure his Remington was ready to use.

Even though it was a short distance, the Apaches came thundering in, war cries piercing the air. They circled the two of them, ignoring the dead bodies on the ground, before stopping. Savage was surrounded and he guessed, in a world of trouble.

One of the Apaches edged his horse forward and stopped not far away from the Drifter. There were no prizes for guessing who he was, with his high cheeks, hell, the whole face and long hair.

'Speak white-eyed dog before you die,' Taza hissed.

Savage looked about at the other Chiricahua before he spoke. They all looked like they wanted to kill him slowly over a low-burning fire.

Nope, definitely not good.

'What do you want me to say?' Savage asked.

'Leave him, Taza,' Naiche almost pleaded with his brother. 'If it had not been for him I would be dead now. Instead, these men are.'

'And soon he will lay beside them,' Taza insisted.

Naiche walked between them and stopped to stare his brother in the eye. 'No, Taza.'

The siblings stared silently at each other until the quiet was broken by Naiche. 'Father would let him go.'

'Father is not here,' Taza said. 'I am.'

Savage tensed as he readied himself to fight. The last thing he wanted to do was kill one of Cochise's sons, but he would if it meant his own survival.'

'What would your father say?' he asked Taza.

'My father would kill you,' Taza spat.

'He didn't a while back when I was talkin' to him over Arizona way.'

The young Apache frowned.

Naiche almost seemed excited when

he asked, 'Who are you?'

'My name is Savage.'

Naiche recognized the name and looked at his brother. 'I know that name. Remember the story father tells us of the white-eye who saved his life many moons past?'

Taza gave a grudging nod. 'Are you this man?'

'I am.'

'Prove it,' Taza snapped. 'Tell the story.'

Savage told them his version of events from years before and when he was finished, Naiche said to his brother. 'See, it is him. He was the man who saved our father's life and now he has saved mine. We must let him go.'

'Where is it you are going?' Taza asked.

'A place called Bad Tooth,' Savage explained. He opened his jacket to show the badge. 'I'm looking for a man there.'

'You ride for white-eye's law?'

'For now,' Savage nodded.

'The place that you go is bad.'

'I'm aware of that.'

'Then why you go?'

'Because it's part of the job that I'm doing and the man I'm after deserves to be hanged.'

'It might be better we kill you now,' Taza surmised.

'I'll take my chances on the town if you don't have any objections?' Savage told him.

'So be it.'

'You might want to put somethin' on the wound your brother has where them fellers tried to scalp him too,' Savage pointed out.

'He is a young fool,' Taza admonished his brother. 'He was warned about riding off on his own. Maybe it would have been better if they had taken his scalp. Then maybe he would learn.'

He looked at his brother and held out his arm. 'Come, we will find your horse and then leave.'

Savage watched as Naiche scrambled

up behind Taza.

'Thank you, Savage,' Naiche said. 'I will remember you.'

'And I you, young chief.'

'You should leave these mountains, white-eye,' Taza grunted. 'There are many of my people about. They will not allow you to live as I have done.'

I've already met them, Savage thought, but said, 'Say hello to Cochise for me.'

Taza gave him a look of disdain and swung his horse about then gave it a brutal jab with his heels and shouted, 'Heyaa!'

Watching the Chiricahua ride away, Savage couldn't help but sigh with relief.

* * *

It was mid-morning the following day when Savage arrived atop a ridge overlooking the settlement of Bad Tooth. From where he sat on his horse, it looked rundown and squalid, the town surrounded by rubbish and stray curs. And what was more disconcerting, the rancid stench that rode the breeze which gusted towards him, made him wrinkle his nose in disgust.

Bad Tooth smelled of excrement and decay. It was a pungent odor that fitted what he saw through his field glasses. Ramshackle buildings, half fallen-down log buildings, canvas tents mostly blackened by filth and grime.

He panned the glasses to the left and they settled upon a man who'd just emerged from a tent. His clothes were dirty and torn. His face was unshaven and Savage could swear that he could smell him from where he was hidden.

The man staggered about briefly and then stopped in the middle of what could be best described as a rocky, rutted trail. It was no street, that was for sure. He dug into his pocket and pulled out what looked to be paper money, then stood there and started to count it.

Behind the man, Savage saw the flap of the tent go back as another man emerged. This one looked to be dressed worse than the first. As he watched the scene unfold, the second man walked purposefully up behind the first man, drew a six-gun from his belt, and shot the man in the back of the head.

The mortally wounded man dropped to the ground. The flat report of the gunshot reached Savage's ears, delayed by the distance. Bending down, the shooter scooped up the bundle of paper money from the ground and tucked it away in his own pocket. He turned forthwith and retraced his steps through the flap of the tent and was hidden from view.

No sooner had he disappeared, two more men rushed out and began to go over the corpse looking for whatever they could, even the dead man's boots.

They too returned to within the tent.

About the scene of violence, other people, both men, and women went about what they were doing as though oblivious to what had just happened.

Savage looked further along the row

of dwellings and watched as a man walked out of a large, ramshackle building, and stood at the edge of the trail. He proceeded to unbutton his fly and relieve himself where he stood. Once finished, he turned and walked back into the building, not bothering to refasten the button. Savage dropped the glasses down and shook his head. Bad Tooth sure was something else.

Suddenly, a piercing scream drifted up from the stinking settlement. Savage raised his glasses again and saw two figures struggling in the center of the encampment. One was a big bear of a man who wore bib overalls and had a headful of unkempt hair. The other was a woman who looked to be part negro.

She wore a drab grey dress and her hair was long and wild. She struggled against the man's grip but couldn't break free. The anger inside of Savage grew as he watched the man strike the woman across the face with a meaty hand. He may not have heard the stinging blow, but the Drifter winced anyway.

The woman's legs buckled briefly and for a moment it looked as though she might fall all the way to the ground. Instead, she made a movement that Savage almost missed. Her right hand went up under her dress and came out holding something.

The brute dragged the woman upright by her hair. Savage could see the pained expression on her face through the glasses. Her head was tilted back and the man crushed her lips with his own.

Savage saw the woman bring up her hand with the object in it. She made a motion that appeared as though she was punching him in the guts with her fist. He staggered back with a look of shock on his face. He clasped a hand to the area and then took it away. He looked at the hand as it came away slick with blood. He lifted his gaze and the woman's hand flashed again. This time it was higher up.

Savage watched as the attacker's clothes changed color, his blood flowing in a torrent down the front of him from the ghastly wound in his throat. He stood stunned for a moment before his legs gave way and he collapsed at the woman's feet.

That was interesting, he thought. As would be going in there after Bobby Vandal. There was a real possibility that he wouldn't come back out.

* * *

While Savage watched over Bad Tooth, Rawhide Allen looked down at a putrefying corpse. Its face was distorted and discolored. The once red blood was now black and the hole from the bullet wound seemed to have a life of its own now that the flies had been at it. Scavengers had taken advantage of the opening in the torso and had been feasting on his insides.

A gust of wind came up and blew the pungent scent of decay into Allen's face. The stink didn't bother him. He'd smelled it all before. It was like an old friend that brought back memories of the war where he reveled in the killing and death it provided. There were often days when he wished that it had never ended.

There were other bodies scattered across the grass, though this was the corpse that interested him the most. This one hadn't been killed by the Indians. Allen didn't know how he knew, but he did. He could feel it.

Which meant that Savage had killed this man. After he'd been scalped, and had his guts slashed open.

Allen smiled coldly. Maybe Savage had a weakness after all. Now, all he had to do was find him and kill him.

It was later in the afternoon when he found the rotting corpses of Jimmy and Rhett. At this rate, Allen figured, he could just follow the trail of dead and they would lead him right to Savage. Maybe he figured wrong earlier. Maybe his quarry would prove to be a very formidable foe.

One thing was certain, at least his ass didn't hurt like a bitch no more.

⋆ ⋆ ⋆

An eerie howl echoed across the darkness as Savage and the pinto approached the settlement of Bad Tooth. He wasn't surprised: the stench coming from the town was enough to attract all manner of scavengers. He was surprised that there were no bears around. Maybe they were more self-respecting than the humans who lived here and found the odor too offensive.

As he entered Bad Tooth, the Yellow Boy lay across his lap ready to use. The badge had been removed and tucked away in Savage's boot.

A man emerged from a tent and stared curiously at him as he rode past. A figure came out of a canvas building farther along and turned down a narrow alley, moving from sight.

Savage climbed down from the pinto

and walked to the dark alley mouth. He followed the man in and had only gone twelve or so feet before he stopped and called after him.

'Hey, you? Got a minute?'

The man stopped and squinted to see the face in the deep shadows of the alley. 'What do you want?'

'I'm supposed to meet a friend of mine here. His name's Bobby Vandal, do you know him?'

The man hesitated which gave him away. 'Um, nope. Never heard the name before.'

'Are you sure?'

'Yep.'

'Maybe if I tell you what he looks like, you might remember,' Savage offered.

'Nope, never seen him afore.'

'But I ain't even told you what he looks like.'

'I don't much care.'

Savage closed the gap between them swiftly. He grabbed the man and rammed the muzzle of the Yellow Boy up under his chin. 'How about you tell me the truth and I'll let you live.'

'OK, OK. He's in the saloon.'

'Where's that?'

'Down further on the left,' the man said.

'Thanks,' Savage said to him and brought the Winchester's butt up in a sweeping blow that dropped the man into a dark oblivion.

He walked out of the alley and took up the pinto's reins. He led the animal along the dimly lit street until he found what he was looking for. The saloon wasn't much to look at. A dilapidated, hastily thrown together affair that needed a lot of attention from what he could see.

Savage tried to tie the pinto's reins to the cross member of the hitch rail but the loose timber fell at his feet with a dull thud. Instead, he had to be satisfied with tying it to one of the wobbly upright posts that were left behind.

Before going in, he checked the loads

in all his weapons. Satisfied they were fine he paused briefly and then walked inside.

7

The makeshift saloon was something . . . Well, it was something almost indescribable. Savage was taken aback by what he saw before him.

He almost tripped over the dead body that lay just through the doorway, and by the look of him, he'd been there for a while. Either they had forgotten he was there or hadn't got around to taking his corpse outside. A large black bloodstain surrounded two holes in his shirt where he'd been shot. His eyes were still open but had turned an opaque, milky white, indicating that he had indeed been there for some time.

Savage screwed his face up at the pungent odor emanating from the corpse and knew that they couldn't possibly have forgotten that he was there. The stench would be a constant reminder. He looked around the room, trying to see Bobby Vandal. No such luck. Instead, a man dressed in tattered clothing called out to him.

'Don't mind, Jed, stranger,' he cackled. 'He don't bite no more.'

The man held up his left hand wrapped in a blackened, bloodstained rag. He smiled, revealing a completely black set of teeth that matched the stains on the rag. He was seated at a lopsided table with another man and a whore. The woman was naked from the waist up and her ample breasts sagged low on her chest. She gave a strained laugh at the man's attempt at humor and revealed a gap-toothed smile.

'You don't belong here,' a woman's soft voice warned him. 'You need to leave while you can.'

Savage looked to his right and to his surprise, saw the woman he'd witnessed kill the man earlier. Up close, under all the grime on her walnut colored face, Savage thought that if she bathed occasionally, she would be quite pretty.

'Thanks for the warning,' he said and

walked towards the bar.

She followed him, a couple steps behind. Once they reached the bar, an unshaven, foul smelling barkeep looked at him and snapped, 'What do you want?'

'What do you have?'

'I got redeye.'

'Then that'll do,' Savage said. He felt the woman move in beside him and he turned his head. She stared at him with big brown eyes, an unasked question obvious to him. He turned back to the barkeep. 'Make it two.'

The barkeep's eyes narrowed as he looked at the woman. 'Get the hell outta here, Connie.'

'I got as much right to be here as the next person, Jud,' she snapped at him.

'Not if I say you don't, now get out. Go and look for business somewhere else.'

'Get the lady a drink, Jud,' Savage said in a low, firm voice.

Jud opened his mouth to protest but something in the stranger's eyes warned him against it. Instead he found a half-empty bottle and two grime-covered glasses and filled them with the liquid. When he was finished, he looked at Savage and said, 'That'll be a dollar.'

'Kinda steep ain't it?' Savage commented.

'Each,' said Jud.

Savage put two dollars down on the rough plank bar and Jud scooped them up as though someone else was after them. The Drifter threw back his drink and stared at Jud thoughtfully. He then grabbed the bottle of redeye by the neck.

Immediately, Jud's hand clamped over Savage's and he said, 'That'll be ten dollars.'

Savage gave him a withering stare and dragged the bottle from his grip. 'I'm sure at the prices you charge, you can let it go.'

There was a look on the barkeep's face that seemed to telegraph his next move.

'If you got a cut-down shotgun under

that counter of yours, I'd keep clear away from it,' Savage warned him. 'Unless you're real fast with it.'

'Hey, Jud!' a man called from along the bar. 'Get me a drink.'

Jud nodded. 'Be right there.'

'Excellent choice, Jud,' Savage said in a low voice. 'It saved your life.'

Savage found a vacant table against a far wall under a dim lamp. He moved the chair so the wall was at his back and took a seat. He placed the bottle and glass on the battered table then took a decent look around the room.

The man who'd called out to him when he entered, now had his face buried between the breasts of the half-naked whore. Another whore sat on the knee of a different customer, nibbling at his ear. In the far corner, sat three big unshaven men, playing cards.

A noise near his table caught Savage's attention and he looked around at the source. A third whore, just as grubby as the other two, and as scantily clothed, plonked herself down in the seat opposite his.

'Buy me a drink, sweet?' she asked, and gave her best warm smile. She rubbed her hand through her blonde hair, attempting to look enticing.

Savage looked at her deadpan and said, 'Maybe all you girls should get together. Between you, there might be a full set of teeth.'

A confused frown settled on her brow. 'What?'

Connie appeared. 'He said you're butt ugly, bugger off, Sally.'

Sally gave Savage an angry look. 'Why you damned son of a bitch. I was just tryin' to be nice to you and you treat a girl like that.'

She stood up, producing a wicked looking knife. 'You bastard, I oughta gut you.'

Savage's hand streaked across the table and locked onto the whore's wrist. Slowly he applied pressure until Sally gasped and dropped it to the table with a dull thud. She cried out with the pain that shot up her arm and when the

Drifter let it go, she remained stiff and unmoved.

Savage saw why the woman was so afraid to move. Connie had her own knife at Sally's throat, and a bead of blood had formed where the point had pierced the skin.

'Let her go, Connie,' Savage said calmly. 'I think she's got the point.'

Connie took the knife away from Sally's throat. Immediately, Sally whirled on her and snarled, 'Bitch, you'll get yours.'

'Get, before I finish the job.'

Sally stormed off and Connie took her seat. 'Friggin' bitch.'

Savage pushed a glass of redeye across the table towards her. She scooped it up and knocked the harsh liquid back without batting an eyelid.

'You're mighty handy with that knife you've got,' Savage pointed out.

'I get by,' Connie said.

'So I noticed earlier today.'

'What do you mean?'

'I saw what you did to that feller that

was harrassin' you.'

'He got what he deserved.'

Savage was about to reply but was cut off by the sound of a ruckus outside the saloon entrance. Muffled curses followed, then five men burst in through the door. Four of the men were dressed in filthy rags, like most in the settlement. The fifth man seemed to be their prisoner.

They shoved him forward into the middle of the room. The man staggered slightly then regained his balance and straightened. Savage drew in a sharp breath at the prospect of things going from bad to worse. Attached to the front of the man's jacket was a United States Marshal's badge.

* * *

There was something or someone out there in the darkness. Rawhide Allen couldn't be sure which, but he felt its presence. Across his lap sat an 1855 Colt 10-gauge revolving shotgun.

He closed his eyes and waited, listening to the sounds of the night that blended together, the snap and crackle of his small fire joining the symphony.

Allen had become aware of the tail he'd picked up, earlier that afternoon. He was reasonably certain that it was human, although it could be animal. Maybe a mountain lion. He figured he'd find out soon.

Suddenly the sounds about him stopped and thick silence blanketed the surrounding area. All he could hear now was his own breathing, loud in his ears.

Still Allen waited.

Now!

His eyes snapped open and the shotgun came up. Out of the darkness, a figure appeared, dangerous, bent on killing the man near the fire.

The Colt roared and its charge slammed into the oncoming Chiricahua warrior. He was stopped in his tracks as the full force of the blast took him in the chest. Allen didn't wait for him to fall. He thumbed back the hammer on the shotgun and turned to his left as another screaming wraith roared out of the blackness.

As the Apache entered the firelight, his painted face seemed to disintegrate as the gun in Allen's hands bucked again. The third Apache came in from his right but there was no time to bring the shotgun to a firing position. He swept the weapon's butt up to meet the charge and as the Indian leaped at Allen, the brass butt-plate stabbed forward into the Indian's face, dropping him instantly.

Lurching to his feet, Allen turned to meet the assault of the next Chiricahua. This one was the biggest of them all and his hands held a battered Spencer. The weapon roared, belching orange flame. The slug hammered into Allen's side spinning him half around, causing him to stagger.

The killer gritted his teeth against the pain and gathered himself. With a howl of glee, the Apache aimed to fire again but a slight hesitation cost him his life as Rawhide Allen took advantage. The Colt cracked and the Apache was thrust back by an invisible hand, crashing to the ground in a bloody tangle of arms and legs.

Fierce, burning pain radiated from Allen's wounded side but he knew it would have to wait for the moment because there was still another Indian left. He would have to examine it later.

A sinewy arm snaked around Allen's throat from behind, locked into position and started to squeeze. The opposite hand held a razor-sharp knife that he prepared to drive deep into the killer's back.

Instead, Allen thrust forward from the hips and, with great strength, threw the Apache forward over his head.

The Chiricahua landed on the low burning campfire, flames and red-hot coals searing the skin and flesh of his back. It brought forth a cry of pain as the Apache rolled off the still burning fire, sending red embers up into the black evening sky. Holding his knife in front of him, the Indian scrambled to his feet with a snarl of rage.

Low and wary, he began to advance on Allen, determined to make him pay. Rage turned to shock when he realized that he wouldn't get to kill the white-eye. In Allen's right fist was a cocked six-gun.

Without hesitation, the killer fired two shots, and both punched into the Apache's naked chest, killing him instantly. Allen reached into his pocket and removed a fresh, fully loaded cylinder and replaced the empty one while he swiveled about scanning for more targets. All his attackers were either dead or down.

He thought about checking his wound, then remembered the unconscious Indian. He smiled cruelly. Grunting in pain when he bent down, he retrieved a fallen knife from the dead Apache nearest to him and looked at it in the low glow of the flickering firelight.

It was time to have some fun.

8

'You have to get out of here now,' Savage ordered Connie in a harsh whisper.

'What are you going to do?' she asked, warily.

'Stop them from killin' that marshal,' Savage told her.

'But why?'

He stared hard at her. 'Because it's the right thing to do.'

'There's a lot of people buried around here that tried to do the right thing,' she warned him.

He watched as the men shoved their prisoner into a chair and one of them punched him mercilessly in the face.

'OK, listen up. I'm only goin' to tell this to you once,' his gaze burned into her. 'I'm the sheriff from Dead Man's Gulch. I'm here chasin' a killer who murdered the previous sheriff among others. However, I ain't goin' to sit by while these sons of bitches kill that marshal. Things are about to heat up and I can't keep an eye on you while I'm watchin' them.'

An indignant look crossed Connie's face. 'Why the hell should you want to keep an eye on me?'

Savage's eyes flared. 'Just shut up and go.'

'Rundown shack at the end of the street,' Connie said, standing up.

'What?'

'It's my place. Just in case you need somewhere to hide.'

'I'll keep it in mind.'

'Yeehaw! Hit that sumbitch again,' a loud voice cried out. 'Ram the bastard's teeth all the way down his throat.'

The Yellow Boy was leaning against a spare chair beside Savage's table. He picked it up and thumbed back the hammer. More blows were landed and blood sprayed from the marshal's face with each one.

One of the captors took out a

large-bladed skinning knife and shouted above the din, 'Hold his head still. I'm goin' to cut his damn ears off.'

A desperate struggle ensued as the marshal fought with all the might he could muster in a fruitless attempt to stop what was about to happen. But it was to no avail. The beating had taken most of his strength.

The man with the knife moved closer and reached out to grab the left ear. Instinctively the marshal pulled his head away.

'I said hold him, damn it,' the knife-wielder cursed.

About the room people started to cheer him on, their bloodlust rising. The man smiled and leaned in again.

Savage knew that if he was going to intervene, now was the time. There would be no reasoning with them. These were violent people who only understood one thing. Violence! He stood up from his chair.

The Yellow Boy roared to life, filling the room with a loud crack. The .44

Henry slug hit the man with the knife, just above his left ear. His head snapped to the side, a large spray of crimson, laced with skull fragments and brain matter splattered over the man beside him. The knife wielder crashed to the floor in a heap.

Shouts of confusion masked the lever action of the Yellow Boy but not the sound of the next shot as it thundered again. This time, the man with the gore splattered face took the full force of the shot as the slug tore a ghastly hole in his throat.

He reached up and tried to plug the spurting wound, but the blood ran freely through his fingers. Within minutes he was dead on the floor.

Savage jacked another round into the Yellow Boy's breech and held his fire. He looked at the stunned men near the marshal and shouted above the remaining noise in the room, 'Everybody freeze!'

They all stopped and looked at the stranger with the buckskin jacket.

'I'll kill anyone who makes a wrong move!' he called above the murmurings. 'I think I've already proved that!'

'What the hell you go and shoot Red and Bob for, stranger?' one of the captors blurted out. 'This ain't none of your concern.'

'It is now. Especially when you're goin' to start cuttin' on a United States Marshal,' Savage told him. 'What sort of dead shit place is this anyway? Look at you all. You're pathetic. Can't even get rid of a dead man outta the doorway.'

There was movement behind the group surrounding the marshal. Savage shifted his aim and squeezed the Yellow Boy's trigger.

Everyone jumped at the deafening sound, but none more than Jud the barkeep. The bullet took him in the chest, punching him back against the makeshift shelves behind his counter, creating a large patch of blood on his shirt. Bottles shattered under the impact and breaking glass added to the cacophony in the room.

From Jud's lifeless hand fell the cut-down shotgun he kept under the counter. Then, as a stunned quiet settled across the small crowd once more, Savage said, 'I'm thinkin' you're all deaf and dumb too.'

'Don't shoot anymore, stranger,' a different man said. 'Just tell us what you want before you kill us all.'

'It's him!' a familiar voice called out. 'He's the feller I told you about. The law-dog that shot down Rhett and Jimmy. All 'cause of a stinkin' Indian.'

The Yellow Boy's aim shifted again and settled on Sheb.

'What did I say would happen the next time I saw you?' Savage asked icily.

At the prospect of his imminent death, a large wet stain appeared on Sheb's pants and the smell of urine wafted up, making those beside him shuffle away.

'Looks to me like you had yourself an accident,' Savage observed.

'Don't shoot me?' Sheb blubbered.

Savage turned his disgusted gaze away from the terrified man and waved his rifle at the crowd.

'Everybody over against the far wall,' he ordered.

They shuffled as one and did as ordered. 'OK. Now I want all guns on the floor. Any funny stuff and you know what will happen.'

While the guns dropped one by one, Savage walked over to the marshal. He looked down at the bloodied face and asked, 'Are you able to get up?'

The man turned his head to look up at Savage. Beneath the crimson mask that covered his face, Savage could see that one eye was already closed, his nose was broken, and his lips were split.

The marshal gave a jerky nod. He leaned forward, spit a glob of blood from his mouth and said, 'I reckon. They didn't break my legs.'

He struggled to his feet.

'I got a horse outside, a pinto,' Savage informed him. 'Wait out there.

I'll be right behind you.'

Once the marshal had exited the stinking establishment, Savage started to walk backward in the same direction, not taking his eyes from those in front of him.

'If anyone pokes their head out the door before we're gone, they'll get up close and personal with a .44.'

No sooner had he passed through the doors, when a chorus of shouts and curses sounded followed by the bumps and thumps of men scrambling for their weapons.

Savage ran for the pinto and hauled himself into the saddle. He reached down and helped the marshal up behind him.

'Thanks for the help,' he said, from behind the Drifter.

'Don't thank me yet. We ain't out of this by a long shot.'

Savage sawed on the reins and brought the horse's head around. He then gave it a couple of hard kicks to set it running along the rutted thoroughfare. The animal had only just lengthened stride when the first shots sounded behind them.

Sharp cracks indicated the passage of bullets that passed close by the speeding animal as it carried its double load.

'Keep your head down!' Savage shouted back to the marshal.

'Don't worry I . . . ' the sentence was cut short by an audible grunt.

The marshal stiffened behind Savage and he realized that the man had taken a bullet. Hurriedly he rammed the Yellow Boy into the saddle scabbard and reached back with his free hand. He grabbed the wounded marshal and called over his shoulder, 'Hang on. Just hang on.'

They raced past the outskirts of the settlement and into the night. An angry voice growled after the hoofbeats had faded away, 'Find them. Find them and kill them.'

* * *

Savage detoured from the trail about a mile from Bad Tooth and found shelter in a thick stand of pines. He dismounted and helped the wounded marshal down. He lay him on the ground and used his hands to check the wound in the dark. It was a waste of time. The only thing Savage successfully did was locate the bullet hole. It was high up on the right side and he was reasonably sure that it had passed through the marshal's lung.

There was no way he could treat something like that out in the open. He needed to get the wounded marshal into a bed and under the care of a doctor. Bad Tooth was the closest settlement and it was certain suicide to return, but he thought of Connie and her offer of sanctuary.

The probability of Bad Tooth having a doctor was slim to none but at least the marshal would be comfortable in a bed.

'I gotta take you back,' Savage said to him. 'Hell, I don't even know your name.'

'It's — it's Sam Fulton,' he rasped.

'Alright, Fulton. I'm Jeff Savage and right now I'm goin' to hurt you again. I need to get you back on the pinto. I'm pretty sure that the bullet passed through your lung. We're goin' back to Bad Tooth to try and find a doctor.'

On cue, the marshal gave a rattling cough.

'You could be right,' he managed to get out. 'But don't go back there on my account. You'll only get yourself killed. I'm done. I can feel it.'

'You let me worry about that,' Savage said to him.

He bent down to help the marshal up but paused as he heard a low rumble in the distance. Savage stood up again and his hand dropped automatically to the Remington six-gun.

Steadily the volume of the rumble increased until the earth around them seemed to tremble. Combined with the numerous hoofbeats, came the snorts of horses and shouts of angry men filtering through the trees. Savage held his breath as the riders galloped past their hidden position and eventually the drum of hoofbeats faded into the night.

'Alright, let's get you back on that horse.'

It took a major effort with a lot of pain to finally get Fulton back on the pinto. Savage climbed up behind him and turned the horse toward the main trail. They paused at the edge of the tree-line and listened.

When there were no more sounds, he edged the pinto out onto the trail and turned towards Bad Tooth. 'Hang on, Fulton, we'll get you some help.'

9

An urgent banging on Connie's door startled her at first.

'Who is it?' she called tentatively, as though afraid of being heard.

'It's me, Savage,' came the voice from the other side.

She hurried to the door and opened it. When she saw the wounded Fulton, she gasped, 'What happened?'

'He got shot while we were tryin' to get away,' Savage told her as he pushed past her. 'Have you got somewhere I can lay him down?'

'Take him over to my bed,' Connie told him.

Connie hadn't been lying when she told him her place was the little rundown shack. He lay Fulton on her bed and turned to face her.

'There wouldn't be a doctor in this

hole in the ground by any chance would there?'

In the orange glow of the candlelight, he saw her face fall. There was no need for her to answer.

'God, damn it!' he cursed loudly.

'Savage?'

The Drifter turned to face the form on the bed. 'I'm here.'

'So I heard. I already told you I'm done. Don't take it personal. You did your best.'

'It weren't anywhere damn near enough,' Savage pointed out.

'It was more than a man could expect under the circumstances,' Fulton said. 'I always expected to die on the job. I don't know how I knew, I just did. In my jacket pocket, you'll find a letter for my sister in Chicago. Can you see that she gets it?'

'I'll take care of it,' Savage assured him.

'Thanks,' Fulton said. 'If you don't mind, I'm tired. I kinda need to sleep.'

'What now?' Connie asked.

Savage shrugged. 'I came here to get a man, a killer.'

'You still aim to do that?'

'Yeah, I guess so.'

'Maybe I can help you,' Connie offered, as she moved towards a rickety table.

He followed her and sat down in a rough chair she proffered. 'Why would you do that?' Then he said, 'No. I'd rather you stayed out of it. I'll work it out on my own.'

'If he's here, you'll need someone to find out where,' Connie pointed out. 'And you can't walk around Bad Tooth now. Not after you went and shot some of its fine, upstanding citizens.'

Frowning, Savage asked, 'How do you know what I did?'

'I watched,' she told him. 'You sure do have a cold streak in you. Why?'

'Mind your own damned business,' he snapped harshly.

Her own gaze grew stony. 'Fine. Do you want my help or not?'

Savage's face softened. 'Sorry. Yes, I'd

appreciate that.'

'Good.'

'But only just to see if the feller I'm lookin' for is still here.'

'Tell me what he looks like, what his name is.'

He gave her the description and other things she needed to know, then Connie stood up and headed for the door.

'Where are you goin'?'

'To find Bobby Vandal,' she said.

'Now?' he asked, in disbelief.

'If I find him now it'll be easier for you to get him out of Bad Tooth with all the searchers combing the surrounding mountains for you.'

It made sense, he thought. 'OK. Be careful, he's a cold killer. He won't hesitate to kill you.'

Connie nodded. 'I'll be back.'

* * *

When Bobby Vandal finished, Cindy rolled her eyes and said a silent thank you as the scar-faced killer flopped down beside her on the lumpy mattress. All the way through their coupling he'd grunted like a pig in her ear. She'd fully expected him to squeal like one when he was done.

Suddenly Bobby sat up and swung his legs over the side of the bed.

'I need a drink,' he announced.

'You and me both,' Cindy murmured.

'What?' Bobby snapped, as he reached for his pants.

'I said, maybe you could buy me one?'

He snorted. 'You got all you're gettin' out of me.'

Son of a bitch.

Once dressed, he left Cindy's one room shack. Deciding that she might as well try to get another customer for the night, she closed the door behind herself and followed him.

When they walked into the saloon, it was almost empty. Someone had gone to the trouble of removing the bodies, though the bloodstains and the damaged shelves behind the counter were still evident.

'Where'd everybody go?' he asked loudly.

'Gone after the two fellers who lit outta here,' replied a bearded man who sat at a corner table.

'They must be important to empty the place out,' Bobby observed.

'You might say that.'

Bobby waited for him to continue but when nothing more was forthcoming, he shrugged and turned to face the bar.

'Did the barkeep go too?' he asked.

'Nope.'

'Where is he then?'

'Dead.'

'Too bad,' Bobby grunted and stepped behind the bar to help himself, his boots crunching on broken glass.

'Who killed Jud?' Cindy asked one of the few working girls that remained.

'Some feller who thought he'd take a hand in some fun that didn't concern him,' she pouted as she explained. 'He just shot Red and Bob down cold. He was some sort of lawman too.'

The drink in Bobby Vandal's hand stopped halfway to his lips. 'What do you mean?'

'The feller Red and the others brought in here was a marshal,' the whore answered. 'They was goin' to cut him up some before they killed him. But then this other lawman feller bought in. He just killed them where they stood. No warnin', nothin'. He cut loose with that rifle of his and killed them, he did. No warnin' at all. Just . . . '

'No warnin', I get it,' Bobby said impatiently. 'What did he look like?'

She shrugged. 'Solid feller, black hair. Wore cavalry pants and a buckskin jacket.'

'Shit,' Bobby cursed.

'Do you know him?' Cindy asked.

'Yeah, I know the son of a bitch,' Bobby nodded. 'His name's Savage.'

'Now, why is it that this feller would

be here interferin' in our lives?' the bearded man asked.

'Because he's after him is why,' Connie said, from the doorway.

Bobby's head snapped about so fast it almost fell off. 'Who are you?'

'More to the point, friend,' the bearded man said, standing up from his seat, 'why is he after *you*?'

Two other men followed suit, dropping their hands to their holstered six-guns. Bobby Vandal swallowed hard. He needed a distraction.

'I'll pay each of you five hundred dollars for your guns,' he blurted out.

They paused. 'You got that much money?' the bearded man asked skeptically.

'I got five hundred on me but I can get the rest when I need it. All you have to do is get me back to Dead Man's Gulch.'

'How do we know if we can trust you or not? What's your name?'

'Bobby Vandal.'

The three men looked at each other

before nodding. They'd heard of Craig Vandal.

'Alright, come daybreak we'll escort you back to Dead Man's Gulch. But you better not be playin' us. Or that lawman will be the least of your problems.'

Bobby turned back to say something to Connie, but she was gone. He frowned.

* * *

'I found him,' Connie said, as she hurried through the door. She pulled up short when she saw the look on Savage's face. 'What is it?'

'Fulton died while you were out,' Savage told her. 'He just stopped breathin'.'

Connie's eyed darted to her bed but it was empty. 'What . . . ?'

'Out back. I thought maybe you could find someone to bury him tomorrow.'

She nodded. 'I can try.'

Savage nodded too. 'Now, you said

you found Bobby Vandal?'

'Yes, he's over at the saloon.'

'Great,' Savage's voice dripped with sarcasm.

'It's not as bad as you think,' Connie explained, 'Most of the men rode out of Bad Tooth looking for you. There are still a few there, but not many.'

'Three.'

'OK.'

'There is one slight problem though,' she said hesitantly.

'Go on.'

'Bobby offered them five hundred dollars each to help him get back to Dead Man's Gulch,' she said.

'When?' Savage asked.

'Tomorrow morning.'

'Then I'd best do somethin' about it,' Savage said.

Suddenly the door burst open, and a tall, angry-looking Negro walked in. His large fist held a cocked six-gun. He lined it up on Savage's chest and snarled, 'I'm goin' to kill you, you son of a bitch.'

10

'Malavai, wait!' Connie exclaimed and inserted herself between the two men. 'It's OK.'

'Get outta my way, Connie, I'm goin' to shoot this sumbitch.'

'It's OK, Mal, he's a friend.'

'Yeah, Mal, I'm a friend, now point that damned six-gun somewhere else before I take it from you and ram it down your throat,' Savage said icily.

'How about I put a bullet in your head for botherin' my sister,' Malavai suggested.

'Enough!' Connie shouted. Then in a calmer voice, she said, 'He's just hiding out here for a while.'

'What?'

'I'm goin',' Savage said. 'I got a date with a killer that ain't goin' to wait.'

He shouldered past a surprised Malavai and walked out the door.

Malavai gave his sister a perplexed look. 'Who the hell was that?'

'His name is Savage,' she told him. 'And he needs your help.'

'Why should I help him?'

Connie went on to explain what had happened while he'd been gone and when she'd finished, the expression on her brother's face was one of uncertainty.

'I still don't see why I should help him,' Malavai stated.

'Because I asked you to,' Connie said.

Malavai thought about it briefly before saying firmly, 'No!'

Then came the sound of distant gunfire.

* * *

As far as saloons went, this one sure was a bloody place, Savage observed of the scene before him. Two men and one of the saloon girls were dead on the filthy floor. Bobby Vandal carried lead in his right shoulder, and the third bodyguard he'd hired, was gasping for breath as his lungs filled with blood. Savage shook his head as a wave of weariness swept over him. He'd been involved in way too much killing of late.

No sooner had he walked through the door when the shooting started. Bobby Vandal took one look at Savage and clawed at his six-gun. He took a slug from the Yellow Boy before he could even clear leather. With him out of action, that left the three men he'd hired as guards.

Taken completely by surprise, the first man took a .44 slug to his chest that incapacitated him straight away. The second man had recovered from his shock and was bringing his sidearm to bear when Savage jacked another round into the breech then fired from the hip.

The bullet flew high of its mark, missing the man's chest but blew through his teeth, splintering them and deflected up into his brain. As the bullet struck home, the man reflexively squeezed the trigger of his six-gun and the shot flew wild. It punched a round hole between Cindy's large pale breasts.

Shock registered upon her face as she looked down at the hole which had begun to leak a stream of crimson. Then her eyes rolled back in her head and she collapsed to the floor.

The third man's gun roared before Savage could get another round into the breech. The slug hit the wall behind Savage with a loud thwack. The thin plank walls proved no obstacle to the bullet which passed through with ease.

The Yellow Boy fired again and the last man was punched back against the wall. Savage let him have a second slug that struck him very close to the first. With a low moan the man slid down the wall, leaving a large blood streak in his wake.

Savage stood there and observed the results of the violent shootout.

'You son of a bitch,' Bobby Vandal grated. 'I'm goin' to damn well kill you.

Friggin' shot me.'

'Shut up,' Savage snapped. 'You're lucky to still be alive.'

The man with the chest wound, the first one he'd shot, coughed a wet gurgling cough. Savage walked across and stood over him. It was the bearded man. A trickle of blood ran from the corner of his mouth, staining his whiskery growth.

'I knew I shoulda minded my own business,' he managed, then died.

Soft sobs interrupted Savage's thoughts and he turned his head and saw a whore with black hair kneeling beside Cindy's body, tears falling on the dead girl's face. She looked up at Savage, her tear-streaked face screwed up with anger.

'Why?' she asked bitterly.

'Maybe she forgot to duck,' he said icily.

'Asshole.'

Movement in the doorway brought Savage around and the Yellow Boy came up into firing position. His finger was stayed, however, by the sight of Connie and her brother Malavai standing there.

'If you've come to help, you're a bit late,' Savage snapped.

'I'll help you get him back to Dead Man's Gulch,' Malavai said.

Savage stared at him for a moment then said, 'I'd appreciate it. But I ain't goin' to Dead Man's Gulch. I'm takin' him to Albuquerque.'

Malavai nodded. 'I ain't doin' it for free. You'll pay me. I want a hundred dollars for the help.'

Nodding, Savage said, 'Fair enough.'

'When do you want to leave?' Malavai asked.

Savage looked at the wounded Bobby Vandal. 'We go now.'

'Hey, what about seein' to my wound?' Bobby protested.

'Shut up. Let's go.'

* * *

Dawn's first light found the three riding steadily along a rocky trail lined with tall pines. The rough path wound its way down a slope strewn with large boulders and at one point it became clear enough for them to be able to see the narrow valley below.

An hour later they arrived at a small creek with a rocky bottom of smooth, round pebbles. They stopped for a short break and allowed the horses to drink.

'Why are you helping me, Malavai?' Savage asked the Negro.

He studied the Drifter for a moment before answering. 'Because Connie asked me to.'

Savage nodded. 'You know, I can do it myself.'

'If I turned back now she wouldn't let me hear the end of it,' he told Savage.

'Yeah, I guess. Tell me somethin'. Why Bad Tooth?'

'It's a rough place, but people generally leave us alone.'

'From what I've seen, I'm not surprised.'

Malavai gave him a puzzled look so

Savage related what he'd seen.

'She sure can look after herself,' Savage said once he'd finished.

'It's good she killed him,' Malavai said. 'If she hadn't, I would've.'

'If you two have finished gabbin', how about one of you takes a look at my wound,' Bobby bleated.

Savage and Malavai looked at each other before the latter said, 'I'll do it.'

A few minutes later, crouched beside the creek to clean the wound, Bobby said, 'I'll give you two thousand dollars to get me outta this.'

Malavai paused, seeming to think hard about the very generous offer he'd been made, then continued to wipe the blood away.

'That's it,' Bobby said, 'think about it.'

Once Malavai was finished, Bobby looked him in the eye and asked, 'Well? Whadda you say?'

Malavai smiled thinly then bunched his fist. He let loose with his massive paw and punched Bobby in his wounded shoulder. The killer doubled over in pain, gasping.'

'Is everythin' OK?' Savage asked.

'Just fine,' Malavai answered. 'We was just gettin' to be friends.'

'Alright. Get him on a horse. We're burnin' daylight.'

A few minutes later, an unhappy Bobby Vandal was back in the saddle, complaining bitterly that his wound hurt. Savage was starting to wish that he'd just killed him in the first place.

* * *

Rawhide Allen rode into Bad Tooth around noon the same day. Once again, he was feeling mean. This time his simmering rage was caused by the festering bullet wound in his hide.

He let his horse pick its way along the rutted street until he reached the saloon. Initially, he wasn't quite sure if he smelled it. Maybe his mind was playing tricks. Another gust of wind confirmed it for him. The all-pervading stench of death was carried on the breeze and he could almost taste it as he breathed it deep into his lungs.

Allen couldn't help but smile as he climbed painfully from his horse. He strode towards the saloon door where the smell seemed to get stronger. Once clear of the threshold and inside properly, he could take it all in and he decided that this was as close to heaven that he would ever get. The smell of death was almost overpowering in the enclosed space. The bodies lay where they had fallen, still.

'Looks like I missed all the fun,' he murmured.

Three men and a woman, mottled skin, laying, sitting in their bodily fluids. The heavy buzz of flies filled the room. Like him, the winged creatures reveled in death.

'Was it you, my friend?' Allen asked aloud, thinking of Savage. 'I bet it was. Did you enjoy the kill? What about the woman? Did you enjoy that too?'

He breathed deeply, savoring the

smell. Movement in the doorway behind him interrupted his moment of ecstasy.

Without turning, he asked, 'What happened here?'

'I — ah — well,' the voice stammered. 'Some son of a bitch lawman shot everyone, to get at a feller he was chasin'.'

Allen turned to stare at the owner of the voice. He was a thin man with sunken cheeks.

'What was his name?'

'I think they called him Savage,' the man said.

'Where did he go?'

'He took the feller he had been looking for and lit out. Him and Malavai Washington.'

'Who is he?' Allen asked, with curiosity.

'He's a Negro feller who drifts in and out from time to time,' the man explained.

'And you don't know where they went?'

'The girl might know,' the man suggested.

'What girl?'

'His sister.'

I'm going to shoot him, Allen thought. 'Where does she live?'

'Here in Bad Tooth,' the man said.

'Where?' Allen asked, testily.

'Do you want me to show you?'

'No, just tell me.'

'Are you sure?'

Son of a bitch! 'Yes, I'm sure.'

The man shrugged. 'OK. She lives in a rundown shack on the edge of town. Thataway.'

The man pointed in the direction Allen needed to go.

'Thank you,' Allen said, and drew his six-gun and shot him.

Five minutes after killing the man who'd helped him, Allen stood outside the shack where Connie lived. He knocked loudly and waited as the woman came to open the door.

As quick as lightning, Allen bunched his fist and brutally punched her in the mouth. Connie staggered back, stunned. The killer forced his way inside and said in a cold voice, 'We need to have a talk.'

11

'I oughta kill you here and now,' Rawhide Allen hissed. A mix of anger and pain thickening his voice. 'Mind you, that knife trick you pulled was damned impressive.'

Connie lifted her battered face defiantly to look her attacker in the eyes. Her lips were puffy and a thin trickle of blood ran from the corner of her mouth. Tears tumbled from her puffy eyes and left streaks through the dirt and blood on her cheeks.

'Go ahead, you gutless bastard.'

Allen shook his head. 'As much as it would give me great pleasure, and believe me it would be a pleasure, I think you might come in handy. So, you'll come with me. But before we go anywhere, you can patch up this knife wound.'

'It's a shame that I never got it into

your throat,' Connie hissed, a little braver now that there was a chance she might get out of this alive.

After Allen had hit her the first time, Connie had gathered herself and stood toe-to-toe with the killer, silently goading him into hitting her again. He obliged, of course, and Connie had gone down once more. When she came back up, her knife was in her hand and she drove it home with all the force she could muster.

Allen had looked down at the knife protruding from his middle and without a word, had pulled it free and thrown it on the floor. Then he hit Connie again.

'Just clean the damned wound before I change my mind and kill you anyway,' he growled.

* * *

The strange but familiar tingling feeling he got right before something bad happened warned Savage that things weren't right. He leaned forward and took the Yellow Boy from the saddle scabbard, jacking a round into the breach. It was the middle of the afternoon and all was quiet. Too quiet.

'What's up?' Malavai asked in a hushed tone.

'Somethin's wrong,' Savage told him, without taking his eyes from the trees about a hundred yards ahead.

'How do you know?' Malavai asked, following suit.

'I used to get these feelin's back in the war when somethin' bad was about to happen,' Savage explained.

'Like now?'

'Yeah, like now.'

Savage dived from the saddle as gunfire erupted from up ahead. Bullets made loud snapping sounds as they passed close. There was a hollow thunk as one of the deadly slugs hit Bobby Vandal full in the chest. A cry of pain came from the young killer as he slid sideways from his saddle.

Malavai followed Savage's lead and

he too dived from the saddle. His shoulder hit the ground hard and pain shot through him, registering in the deep recesses of his brain. He ground his teeth together and came up with his rifle, ready to fire. Before he had a chance to squeeze the trigger, a bullet slammed into his lower rib area and knocked him out of the fight.

The fingers of pain began to spread from Malavai's wound throughout his body, and he doubled up in a futile attempt to try to ease it.

Once Savage had hit the rocky ground, he rolled off the trail to his left. He then lay on his belly and brought the Yellow Boy into position and let loose with four fast shots. Not really bothering to aim, the gunfire was more to get them thinking. Put them on the backfoot and give himself time.

'Malavai, are you OK?' Savage shouted, snapping off another shot.

'I'm hit,' a pained voice called weakly.

'Damn it,' Savage hissed, as bullets kicked up small eruptions of dirt around him. 'Hang on.'

Savage looked about him. There was an outcrop of rock to his right. If they could get amongst it then at least they'd have better cover.

'Can you hear me, Malavai?'

'Yeah,' came the muffled reply.

'Get ready. This is goin' to hurt.'

'What?'

Savage waited for the next flurry of shots to pass before moving. When he did, however, there was no turning back. He leaped to his feet with the Yellow Boy in his left hand. He then rushed across to Malavai's side and without pausing, grabbed him by the collar and began to haul him towards the rocky outcrop.

Disregarding the pained protests behind him, Savage reached the rocks amid a hail of lead slugs and dropped down beside Malavai.

'I'm goin' to kick your ass for that,' Malavai warned him.

'And I'll be glad to let you,' Savage told him. 'Just let me have a look at this wound of yours first.'

A cursory examination revealed only one hole, the bullet still in there. He turned his gaze to Malavai. 'You'll be fine for the moment. I've got to deal with these bushwhackers.'

'Get my six-gun for me, I'll help out,' the wounded man offered.

Savage shook his head. 'You stay right there.'

More shots flew in their direction, a few smacking loudly into the solid surface of their cover before howling off into the surrounding wilderness.

Savage fired a return volley and ducked back. The rock was peppered with continuous rounds. Keeping low, he peered around the edge of their cover. He saw movement in the treeline as two men crept forward under the cover of constant fire.

He lined his foresight on the closest one and pulled the trigger. The man disappeared behind a puff of blue-gray smoke and when it cleared, he was gone.

Renewed, heavier gunfire rocked the surrounding high-country as the downed man's friends cut loose, forcing Savage to dart back behind the outcrop.

'You done went and upset them, din' you,' Malavai gasped, between waves of pain.

'Some,' Savage acknowledged.

Before he knew it, they began to take fire from the left, indicating that someone had flanked them. Savage dropped to the ground as angry lead hornets fizzed past his ears.

'Damn it,' Savage cursed. 'Give me a break. Ever since I rode into this territory, some bastard has been tryin' to kill me.'

'Maybe you should leave then,' Malavai said, pain etched in his voice.

'Just what I aim to do,' Savage called across to him. 'Providin' I don't wind up dead first.'

'Do me a favor?' Malavai asked.

'What?' Savage asked as another slug passed close by, making him flinch.

'Look after Connie for me? If I don't make it.'

'Shut up, you'll be fine.'

Suddenly the shots changed. They didn't stop but ceased coming at them. Savage heard the gunfire continue but . . .

He cautiously edged around the outcrop again and saw that the bushwhackers had emerged from the trees. They were still firing their guns in the opposite direction. Savage looked further out and saw why. From the trees had emerged a bunch of Apaches.

Savage recognized Taza leading them. Out front, his sturdy pony aimed straight at a fleeing white man. The Drifter could almost hear the sickening sound as Taza's horse rode over the bushwhacker, the horse's hoofs turning the man's skull to a crushed and bloody mess.

The end came swiftly for the remaining bushwhackers. The handful of Chiricahua warriors dispatched them with efficiency and the last of them fell with an arrow through his throat. With wild cries of excitement, the warriors leaped from the backs of their horses and started their brutal work on the fallen.

All except Taza. He pointed his dappled pony towards Savage and Malavai's hiding spot. He drew up short and said, almost disdainfully, 'We meet again white-eye.'

Savage came out from behind the rocks, rifle in his hands. He was wary of the Apache, just in case his blood was too far up and he had designs on his scalp too.

'It seems that it is my hide being saved this time,' Savage observed.

Taza nodded. His eyes then drifted across to the wounded Malavai.

'Will he die?' he asked bluntly.

'Not if I can get him to a doctor,' Savage told him.

Again, Taza nodded. Then, without another word, he turned his horse away and rode back to join the rest of the Apaches. Savage heard some muffled words and the Indians mounted their horses and followed Taza back into the trees.

After they were gone, Savage checked on Malavai. He looked up at the Drifter with pain filled eyes and said, 'That was convenient.'

'Wasn't it though,' Savage agreed. 'Now, we need to get you to a sawbones.'

'What about Bobby Vandal?' Malavai asked.

Bobby Vandal!

'Hell, I'd clean forgot about him,' Savage acknowledged. 'Don't go anywhere.'

'Funny man aren't you?' Malavai snorted, then winced as more pain shot through him.

Savage found Bobby face-down in the grass beside the trail. There was a gaping, red hole in his back where the bullet had burst through from the other side. The Drifter couldn't tell if he was still alive or not, so he leaned down and rolled the young killer over.

Bobby Vandal's face was sickly gray and a thin line of blood ran from the corner of his mouth. His eyes fluttered open and he smiled weakly.

'You . . . You're . . . dead man,' he choked out, his voice a wet gurgle.

'Not anytime soon,' Savage said grimly. 'You, on the other hand, ain't got much longer for this world. Seems quite fittin' really.'

Bobby's slowly dimming eyes flashed. He opened his mouth to speak but all that came out was a wet cough. More blood followed and his head lolled to the side.

Savage nodded. 'See you in Hell.'

'Is he dead?' Malavai asked when Savage returned.

'He is now,' Savage confirmed. Then he said, 'I'm goin' to hurt you again. I need to get you onto that horse of yours and back to Dead Man's Gulch. There'll be a doctor there who can check you over.'

'What about Craig Vandal?' Malavai asked.

'Well, I guess that seein' I'm still the only law in town, I'll have to tackle that problem when it arises,' Savage said. 'And with his son bein' dead, I think it's about to get mighty interestin'. Don't want a job, do you?'

Malavai gave him a pained smile. 'Get me on that damned horse before I die laughin'.'

Savage got him onto his horse and moved off to lift and tie the body of Bobby Vandal across the saddle of the third horse. Before they started out, he looked the horses over and, not satisfied, he went back and secured Malavai to the saddle so he wouldn't fall.

'Why don't you just tie me across the saddle and be done with it?' Malavai moaned.

'Are you ready?' Savage asked, ignoring the inference.

Malavai nodded.

'OK then, let's go.'

12

Savage kept them riding through the night and most of the next morning, afraid that lifting Malavai in and out of the saddle would do more bad than good. Not that all the riding would help his condition anyway.

They rode into Dead Man's Gulch an hour before noon, people staring at the small party as it made its way along the street. Savage eased the horses up to the hitch rail in front of the jail and climbed down.

'You,' he called to a fair-haired man.

'Me?' the startled man asked, eye-brows raised.

'Yeah, you. Is there a doctor handy in town?' Savage asked.

'Ah, yeah.'

'Good, go get him.' Savage watched the man hurry away then singled out another two. 'You, go find someone who can bury this damned body.'

'Is that . . . ?' the wide-eyed man with black hair asked.

'Yeah, go.'

'Holy smokes,' he breathed and took off.

Savage then turned to the third man. He was solidly built and looked capable. 'Give me a hand to get my friend here inside.

The man screwed up his face. 'He's one of *them*. Get him down yourself.'

Savage gave him a cold stare. 'Seriously? I tell you what, if you don't help me get him inside, he won't be the only one needin' to see a doctor. Now get your damned ass over here.'

'Untie me, Savage,' Malavai grated. 'I'll damn well walk.'

'Shut up,' Savage snapped. 'You couldn't stand, let alone walk.'

The man still hadn't moved. 'Get your ass over here. Last chance.'

Grudgingly, the man walked over to the horses and helped Savage get Malavai down. They got him inside and as they crossed the room to the cell, Malavai said, 'Looks like you've had some trouble here already.'

'Disagreement with the local bully,' Savage told him.

'Craig Vandal wields a lot of power around here,' the man who was helping said.

'Yeah, well all that's about to come to an end,' Savage stated angrily. 'He'll toe the line or he'll be buried alongside his son.'

'Are you sure about that?' the man asked.

'Are you scared of him?' Savage asked.

'Not a man in his right mind around here who ain't,' the man said.

'And that is what you will have to deal with in this town,' the doctor said, as he passed through the doorway. 'Who's the patient?'

Savage indicated to the bunk. 'Malavai.'

The doctor walked past and began to check out the wounded man.

'I see you got your man,' another newcomer said, as he entered. Judge Perry McArdle looked happy as he stopped in front of Savage. 'Have much trouble?'

Apaches, outlaws, killers, hired guns. Savage shook his head. 'Not a lot. Some.'

McArdle nodded. 'You should know that Craig Vandal hired a killer to go after you. A man named Rawhide Allen. Ever heard of him?'

Pausing for a moment while he flicked through the deepest recesses of his mind, Savage tried to recall the name. 'Can't say as I have.'

'He's a brutal man,' McArdle explained. 'It is said he kills for the pure enjoyment of it. When he's not hired to kill a man or woman for that fact, he kills because he wants to.'

'I guess it goes to show then, don't it?' Savage observed.

'What does?' McArdle asked.

'That things get worse before they get better.'

Then, as if on cue, a howl of anguish

sounded out front of the jail.

'Sounds like we're about to find out,' McArdle said.

* * *

When the door to his office opened, Craig Vandal looked up from the reports in front of him and noticed the worried expression on the lined face of the man who'd entered. He closed the door behind himself and walked over to the desk.

'What is the problem now, Ellis?' Vandal's voice was tired. He held up a hand. 'No, don't tell me. I don't want to know. Just go, I'll deal with it tomorrow.'

Ellis didn't move. Vandal looked up at him and anger flared in his eyes as he quickly lost patience. 'Damn it. I said I'd deal with it tomorrow.'

'I heard you,' Ellis told him.

'Well then, get out.'

'There's somethin' you need to know,' Ellis said, gravely. 'Savage just rode back into town.'

A cloud of rage darkened Vandal's face. 'That bastard just won't go away and die. Get some of the men together. I'll deal with it myself.'

Again, Ellis didn't move.

Vandal gave the man a withering stare but he remained still, having gotten used to his boss' moods over the past couple of years.

'He wasn't alone. He had a wounded Negro with him and a body draped over another horse.'

Vandal froze as an icy chill ran through him. 'Was it Allen?'

'No. It's Bobby.'

'Is he . . . ?' not wanting to know the answer, Vandal let his voice trail away.

'Dead? Yeah. I'm sorry Mr. Vandal. He is.'

Craig Vandal slumped back in his chair. His face paled and he felt as though he'd taken a hammer blow to his guts.

'Are . . . are you sure?' he stammered.

Ellis nodded. 'I checked him myself before I came here.'

A heavy silence descended over the room as Craig Vandal struggled with the devastating news of his son's death. The tick of a clock sounded deafening in the extended quiet.

Then Vandal asked, 'Where is he?'

'Outside the jail, waitin' for the undertaker.'

More silence.

'What do you want to do?' Ellis asked.

Vandal got up from his chair in silence. He walked towards the door and opened it. Then he went out onto the street. Steadily, one foot after the other, he trudged towards the sheriff's office. Seeming as though in a sleep-walking trance, he stared ahead at the corpse still draped over the horse outside the jail.

Onward Vandal walked, his boots scuffing along in the dirt of the street, his gait rigid. As he drew nearer his son's body, he slowed and when he was no further than ten feet from his boy, he emitted a low keening sound from somewhere deep within. It grew louder until a wail erupted from his lips.

Vandal turned to face the jail and shouted, '*I'm going to kill you, you son of a bitch!*'

* * *

Rawhide Allen spat on the ripening corpse of a scalped man with an old, bloodstained rag wrapped about his hand. His eyes were gone; the birds had taken them first and the small critters had started their work too. Not that food was at a premium. There were other corpses scattered about for them to feed on.

'It would seem our friend leads a charmed life,' Allen murmured. He looked over at Connie who was tied to the saddle of a bay horse he'd found unattended in Bad Tooth. As they'd been walking away with it, the horse's owner had appeared.

The man had tried to protest but Allen was in no mood to bandy words. With a total disregard for the niceties of ownership, Allen shot him where he stood.

'I do love the thrill of the hunt,' he said, smiling coldly.

'I hope he kills you,' Connie growled defiantly.

Her words brought the pain of his wounds to the front of his mind. They throbbed nonstop, eating away at his insides. Allen had the telltale sheen of sweat on his brow and his face was already turning a pasty color. He looked about the surrounding landscape, bathed in the bright morning sunlight. Then his gaze shifted back to Connie.

'If I die, it won't be him who'll kill me,' he said to her.

* * *

Savage walked outside the jail holding the Yellow Boy across his body, hammer cocked and ready to use.

Craig Vandal looked at him through tortured eyes.

'You murdering bastard.' He snarled. 'I'll kill you for this.'

'I didn't kill your boy,' Savage told him. 'I was takin' him to Albuquerque for trial when a bunch of fellers jumped us. They were the ones responsible.'

'No. No, they weren't. It was you. Ever since you came here, you've been nothing but trouble. His death is on your head. You should have kept your nose out of it. Now, it's about to get cut off.'

Ellis stood beside him and Vandal made a desperate lunge at the gun he wore on his hip. The gun in Savage's hands swung about and he snapped off a shot. The roar of the Yellow Boy and the fountain of dirt that spewed up near the distraught man's feet stopped his reckless move.

'The next one will kill you,' Savage warned him. 'I'll let this one slide for the fact he was your boy. Even if he was no good. I won't be so forgivin' next time.'

Vandal stood there, visibly shaking with rage.

'Go home, Craig,' McArdle said quietly. 'Take your boy and bury him. You know he got what was comin' to him.'

'*He was my son!*' Vandal roared.

'Who was no good,' McArdle said. 'Take him and bury him. Just let it go.'

There was a drawn-out silence and then Vandal nodded. 'You're right. He should be buried.'

'Now you're thinking clear,' McArdle said.

Vandal's hard-eyed stare burned into Savage and he growled, 'When it's done, I'll be back for you. And if I have to tear this town apart to get to you, I will.'

'I'll be waitin',' Savage said to him. 'But if you do, don't expect to walk away. I already told you, the next time, I'll kill you.'

Vandal tried to stare Savage down

but he wouldn't be drawn. Instead, the Drifter turned away and walked back inside the jail. Blazing eyes burned into his back as Vandal stood there, plotting how to kill him.

I'll kill you, you son of a bitch. Even if it takes until my last breath, I'll kill you!

* * *

When Savage and McArdle went back inside, the doctor had finished with Malavai.

'How's he doin'?' Savage asked.

The doctor looked at Savage through tired, gray eyes and shook his head.

'Damn it. How long?'

'Maybe a couple of days.'

Savage nodded. 'Thanks, doc.'

After his departure, a long silence ensued that was eventually broken by McArdle.

'Do you want a deputy to help you out?' he asked. 'Might be a wise move.'

'Would you be able to find someone?'

Savage asked him.

A thoughtful silence hung in the air as McArdle wracked his brain to come up with a name.

'Yeah, thought as much,' Savage said.

'I could try,' McArdle said, hopefully.

Savage shook his head. 'I'll deal with it. I don't want anyone gettin' killed on my account.'

'But you won't stand a chance on your own,' McArdle said, shaking his head in disbelief.

'I'll get by,' Savage assured him. 'Don't worry.'

13

Craig Vandal presented a forlorn figure, standing over the open grave of his son, as rain poured over him and into the hole at his feet. The leaden clouds had moved in on cue and the storm arrived to mark the somber occasion. He was the only one there. He didn't want others. He'd organized with the undertaker and preacher to have the service done as soon as possible.

Bobby's body had arrived back in town that morning and his burial was held by midafternoon.

Many would question the rush. Craig Vandal now had things to take care of and they wouldn't wait. Lightning brightened the afternoon gloom and a crash of thunder sounded overhead.

Vandal's face was set like stone, cold, unfeeling. He just stared down into the void that had swallowed the rough-hewn plank coffin containing his son.

Then suddenly he turned away and walked back toward town. By the time, he reached the main street, the downpour had stopped. Vandal's boots squelched through several inches of mud that had replaced the dusty surface of earlier in the day.

When Vandal entered the Down and Out saloon, he found the few that remained of his crew, waiting for him. He crossed the floor to the bar, his soaked clothes leaving a trail of water droplets on the dusty planks as he went. Breasting the bar, he looked at the barkeep expectantly.

'Get me a bottle of whiskey,' Vandal demanded.

The barkeep reached under the counter and brought out a nearly full bottle of brown liquid. He placed it on top and sat a glass beside it. Vandal poured himself a drink while the barkeep stood there waiting for payment.

Vandal looked at him sardonically

then threw the drink back, ignoring the man's stare. Then he turned away and sought out Ellis. He caught the man's eye and said, 'Get them together. It's time.'

* * *

McArdle was in the middle of an early supper when they found him in the café. The rain had stopped as he'd headed along to eat and the late afternoon air felt crisp and clean. His order of steak and potato had arrived, and he was looking forward to the pie he'd ordered for dessert.

As McArdle slopped up the last of the gravy with a slice of bread, Vandal entered with three of his men. The boss' gaze settled on the judge and he nodded in that direction. 'There he is. Go get him.'

They rushed forward before McArdle could react. He was grabbed by the arms and dragged, protesting loudly, from his seat.

McArdle began to struggle in earnest. He broke one arm free and lashed out at the man holding his other one. It was a feeble effort and the men regained control and soon had his arms pinned again. Short of patience, Craig Vandal stepped forward, a six-gun in his fist. To the shock and surprise of most of the witnesses in the diner, the gun rose and fell and the judge's struggles ceased.

'Get the old bastard out of here,' Vandal snarled.

'Now wait a minute,' a man said in protest as he stood up from a nearby table. He moved in front of them before they could take McArdle outside. 'You can't just beat a man and take him like that.'

Vandal's demeanor was becoming fouler and he was in no mood for defiance. He raised his eyebrows and said, 'No?'

'No.'

The gun in Vandal's fist came up. He cocked it and shot the man in the head.

The sound of the shot slammed loudly against the walls and the man fell to the floor in an untidy heap. Vandal stood motionless and he stared down at the body as a thin wisp of gun smoke curled lazily upwards from the end of the barrel.

There were shouts and cries from the terrified diners, which he ignored.

'You are not going to stop me,' Vandal growled. He turned his attention back to his men. 'Get him out. You know what to do.'

He followed them out. It was time for the next part of his plan.

* * *

'*Savage! You murdering son of a bitch, get out here!*'

'I guess he means you,' Malavai said, from his bunk.

Savage had thought the man was asleep. He walked over to the cell and looked through the open door.

'How are you feelin'?' he asked.

'Funnily enough, for a dyin' man, I don't feel too bad.'

'*Savage!*'

'Sounds like he means business,' Malavai said.

'It sure do, don't it?'

Savage crossed the room and looked out the glassless window. On the other side of the street stood Craig Vandal and ten of his men. A gloom had settled over Dead Man's Gulch with the late afternoon as the last vestiges of light faded.

'*Savage! Come on out here and get what's coming to you!*'

As Savage looked on, he saw Vandal turn to speak with his men. A second later they all brought up their weapons and opened fire. The thin, plank front wall of the jail, already pockmarked with holes from the last episode, was once again peppered with shots, the bullets punching through to spray fine timber splinters across the room. Savage dived to the floor.

'Son of a bitch,' he cursed and

crawled across the floor to the desk where his Yellow Boy rested on top.

He reached up and retrieved it, a slug passing so close to his hand he felt the heat of its passage.

'Are you OK, Malavai?' Savage called above the noise.

The muffled voice came from the cell. It was inaudible but at least it proved that Malavai was still alive.

With a shattering crash, the lantern on the desk was hit and knocked to the floor. The glass broke and its contents leaked out and caught fire. Flames sprang up, chewing hungrily at the spreading fuel.

'Shit,' Savage cursed again, knowing that he needed to put the thing out before the place burned down around his ears.

Suddenly, the gunfire stopped and an eerie silence ensued, punctuated by the sputtering of the fire as it tried to take hold.

'Are you OK, Malavai?' he called out.

'I'm still here, although you might

need a new bucket for your prisoners to piss in.'

'That'll be the least of our problems if I can't get this fire out,' Savage told him.

'Let it burn.'

'Not yet.'

While Savage was putting out the fire, Vandal called out again, 'Are you still alive in there, you murdering bastard?'

Savage crossed to the empty window frame. He peered out and saw Vandal and his men standing across the way.

'I'm still here,' Savage called back.

'Are you coming out or do we come in after you?'

'What's the difference?' Savage shouted. 'You want to kill me either way?'

'True,' Vandal conceded. 'But I also want to do it where everyone can see. I want to kill you publicly. Not hidden away where I can't watch you die.'

'Why don't you come on over then?' Savage suggested.

'I don't believe that I will,' Vandal

said. 'I would much prefer it if you came out here. But, never mind. Maybe this next demonstration will change your mind.'

There was a flurry of movement and a battered looking Judge McArdle appeared. Wrestled into place by two large men. A third man held a large coil of rope, most of which he dropped into the muddy street. One end had a loop that he placed over the judge's head and drew tight around the throat. He reached down and picked up the other end of the rope, leaving the rest of the coil undisturbed.

'Let him go, Vandal,' Savage called out. He would have shot Vandal then, but the man had placed himself behind the judge and presented no target.

No answer was forthcoming from Vandal, however, the drumming of hoofs on the churned-up street caused Savage to frown. He brought the Yellow Boy into a firing position and waited to get a bead on Vandal. The sound grew louder and the judge's struggles grew more frantic.

The rider came into view and rode past at a good clip, taking the end of the rope from the judge's captor. As the horse disappeared, Savage noticed something that made him freeze. He blinked and thought, *No, that's not right*. He watched in horror as the rope fed out and snapped taught.

For a long time, he would never forget the look of fear on Perry McArdle's face in the moment before the rope cut through his throat with such force, his head seemed to leap from his shoulders in a large spray of blood.

What remained of the esteemed judge, collapsed to the ground while his head rolled into the center of the street. With a roar, Savage opened fire with his Winchester.

The first slug was aimed at Vandal, but a man trying to avoid the spraying blood from the headless corpse stepped across in front of him. The bullet took him in the throat and ripped a gaping wound. The man clasped both hands around it trying to staunch the flow of blood, but it pumped through his fingers and down his shirtfront, turning the blue cloth dark.

Another round was levered into the breech and Savage snapped off his next shot. Across the street, there was panic as they all scrambled for cover. Maybe they'd forgotten he was armed, or perhaps ignorant to the fact that they'd just lost one of their own. Well, they were about to learn the hard way.

The Yellow Boy bucked a third time and a second man hit the ground, the lower part of his face missing. Savage worked the lever once more and fired. A third man screamed and fell to his knees, a .44 Henry slug buried deep in his guts. By this time, the rest of them had managed to escape into the safety of the building across the street, leaving the gravely wounded man kneeling out front.

Savage stopped firing and a semi-silence ensued. He could hear muffled voices across the way, and then the wounded man called to his friends.

'Ollie! Ollie! You gotta help me. I'm gut-shot. The bastard gut-shot me!'

His pleas were ignored.

'Damn it, Ollie, help me! My guts is comin' out! God, it hurts!'

Movement from the doorway directly behind the mortally wounded man caused Savage to raise the rifle and sight along the barrel. It wasn't one of Vandal's men, but a townsperson who had emerged. A man, maybe a store-keeper by the look of him with an apron and a string-tie.

The man paused and turned to look back the way he'd just come. There were some muffled sounds and the man started to walk towards the jail. His steps were hesitant at first, but he began to hurry as he got closer to his goal.

Then, when he was about twenty feet from the jail, a voice from across the street shouted, 'That's far enough!'

The man froze, the look on his face somewhere between terror and anguish. His eyes were wide and as he looked in through the broken window where Savage stood, he begged, 'Help me, please.'

Vandal's voice sounded again from across the way. 'Can you hear me, Savage?'

'I hear you,' Savage called back.

'His life is in your hands,' Vandal shouted. 'Come on out and he'll live.'

'I ain't comin' out,' Savage shouted back. 'But I'll tell you this, Vandal. The law ain't goin' to hang you. It won't get a chance because I'll kill you before it gets that far.'

'Please, you've got to help me,' the man begged again.

'Did I hear you right?' Vandal asked. 'Did you say that you weren't coming out?'

'I did,' Savage called to him. He shifted his gaze to the petrified man and said, 'Run.'

'What?'

‘If you want to live, run damn it,’ Savage snapped and brought up the Yellow Boy.

The thunder of shots rolled along the street as the Drifter worked the lever and fired as quickly as he could, peppering the front of the building across from the jail.

Savage glanced at the retreating form of the man and thought that he might make it. But when the hidden guns opened fire, they were not aimed at him, but at the fleeing man. As he watched on, Savage saw the man struck by at least four bullets before falling to the ground.

Cursing, Savage fired wildly across the street at the building, his anger at the man’s pointless death raised. In his frustration, he took deliberate aim at the mortally wounded man clutching at his middle, trying to keep his guts in, and shot him through the head.

The killing of their man brought forth another hail storm that ripped through the paper-thin walls, causing

Savage to dive onto the floor once again. He felt the burn of lead across his back and he bit back a yelp of pain. Another slug chewed large wooden splinters from the office desk while another smashed into the half-empty coffee pot, sending it clattering to the floor.

Keeping low, Savage crawled across to the jail cell where Malavai was. He passed through the open door as lead fizzed above him. Once he reached the wounded man, one look was all it took to confirm that he was dead.

A bullet had punched into the side of Malavai's head, just above his ear, killing him outright. His eyes were open and his jaw slack. Savage lay there quietly and considered his options.

An overwhelming desire to kill Vandal and his men burned deep within him and it took every ounce of his willpower to prevent himself from doing something rash and more than likely get himself killed. Instead, Savage lay flat while more rounds buzzed around him, as he tried to regain control of his emotions.

When the firing died down, he decided it was time to go. He planned to mask his retreat. He looked at Malavai and said, 'Sorry about this, but you're goin' to go out in a blaze of glory.'

When the firing finally ceased, Savage worked quickly and soon had another fire burning. He crossed to the broken front window and peered out. It was almost dark outside which was good. He would use the cover of it to get away. Not that he planned to go far. He still had too much to do, and Craig Vandal was the subject of all of it.

14

'Hey, look! The jail is on fire!' a man called out, an orange glow evident in the empty space of the window. 'I can see the flames.'

Craig Vandal pushed aside one of his men looking on from one of the windows, so he could get a clearer look. Sure enough, he saw the glow and then the flicker of a flame.

No! Not this way you son of a bitch! I want to see you die, to kill you myself.

'Get to the jail!' Vandal shouted at his men. 'Get him out of there. I want him alive!'

Ellis stood firm, not sure what they were being told to do.

'What?' Vandal snapped.

'Why not let him burn?'

'Because I want him alive,' Vandal snapped.

'If we go chargin' over there, it's us

who're likely to die,' Ellis pointed out.

From inside his jacket, Vandal produced his six-gun, leveled it at Ellis, and squeezed the trigger. The roar was deafening in the close confines of the room and Ellis staggered back from the hammer-blow to his midsection. His stunned expression turned to confusion as it dawned on him that his boss had just shot him.

Craig Vandal wasn't done yet. His frustration and pent-up rage began to overflow in an unstoppable tide. He screamed like a madman as he emptied the gun into Ellis, each bullet strike causing the man to stagger back as it smashed into him. The last one cannoned Ellis into the wall behind him, where he hung suspended briefly, then slid down the wall, dead.

Spinning about, Vandal glared wildly at the others in the room. Recent events had become too much and the man had cracked in a spectacular fashion.

'*Get over there and get him! Now!*' he screeched maniacally.

If events hadn't been so dire, their scrambled exit through the door could have been considered comedic. They pushed and shoved each other, not wanting to fall prey to the wrath of a crazy man.

The first few out into the gloaming, ran into a storm of lead as Savage unleashed a barrage of fire. The gunshots seemed to meld into one, and when they ceased, three men were out of action. The remaining men had split left and right to avoid the killing ground. They found shelter and began to return fire.

Over the din of battle, a voice could be heard screaming, '*Hold your fire, damn it! I said I wanted him alive! Hold your fire!*'

Their gunshots fell away then ceased altogether. Even the gunfire from the jail had stopped. A mesmerizing sight, the flames crept slowly higher as the still-green planks of the recently constructed building retarded the passage of the fire. The smoke produced was thick and smelled strongly of tree sap. The roof caught alight and the intensity of fire increased, illuminating the street in both directions with its eerie orange glow.

Craig Vandal walked outside and stood, watching the inferno. He knew that there was no way in hell that his men would be able to get Savage now. The glow of the flames in the near dark chased the shadows from his face and caused his eyes to sparkle.

Vandal's jaw set firm as he came to terms with the fact that he wouldn't personally get to kill the man responsible for the death of his son. But by hell, the bastard would be dead, and that was all that mattered.

As he watched, the jail's roof succumbed to the inevitable and collapsed, tossing up a cloud of smoke and bright twinkling embers. A thin smile came to Craig Vandal's lips and he said mirthlessly, 'Burn in Hell you son of a bitch. May the Devil get your soul.'

* * *

After his frontal attack had taken out the three, Savage scrambled for the back door, thankful to find it unguarded. From there he turned left and kept to the shadows, making his way further along until he found a large canvas tent used as a laundry. He paused to listen intently to the shouts coming from the street, now that the gunfire had ceased.

The graze on his back still burned, even more so now with sweat seeping into it. He heard the crash of the jail's roof falling in and saw the plumage rise into the air. Edging around the corner of the laundry tent, Savage watched as the remainder of Vandal's men stood in front of the burning jail.

Vandal called them over and spoke briefly, then turned away and walked towards the saloon. Accompanying him were two of his men. They disappeared into the Down and Out and Savage turned his attention to those still on the street. The men were beginning to organize folk who'd come out to look, to assist with the wounded and the fire.

With their attention elsewhere, Savage crossed the street unseen, the Yellow Boy held firmly in his right hand. He slipped down a narrow alley between two tents and around the back. In the shadows of a timber building, he stopped and reached into his jacket pocket. The muffled clink of .44 cartridges sounded loud in the darkness as he dug some out and reloaded the rifle's magazine.

With a round under the hammer, Savage continued silently until he reached the saloon. He found the back door and edged it open. The entrance was near the end of the bar and as he peered in through the crack, he could see Vandal sitting alone and one of the men who'd gone with him sat at a table to the right. That left the other man. Not perfect, but acceptable.

The door went all the way back and Savage stepped into the room. Roy, the barkeep, was behind the bar pouring a drink for the second man that had been with Vandal.

Roy's eyes grew wide, warning the hired gun in front of him. The man whirled on the spot, his hand streaking to the gun at his side. His fingers had only just started to wrap around the weapon's butt when the Yellow Boy thundered and a blossom of red appeared on his chest.

The slug blew him backward in front of the bar until his legs gave out and he slumped to the floor. Roy flinched involuntarily and spilled rotgut on the counter. Then he ducked down low attempting to stay out of the firing line.

The sound of a round being jacked into the chamber was covered by the echo of the first shot. Savage shifted aim and settled the foresight on the man sitting by himself. The man, however, was already on his feet. The chair had flipped over when he'd stood up, and in his hand, was a cocked six-gun.

The man's burning desire to stay alive had given him an almost inhuman speed in drawing his gun, which exploded into life. It bucked hard in his fist but the bullet flew wide, hammering into the wall. The man had sacrificed accuracy for speed which was about to prove fatal.

The bullet from Savage's rifle slammed into him, knocking him backward over the upturned chair. As he fell, his next shot went into the ceiling, raining debris upon a nearby table.

That left Craig Vandal.

He sat at his table, unmoved by the violent deaths of those around him. He looked at Savage through passive eyes and said, 'I had a feeling that you weren't dead. I'd hoped you were but something told me you were still alive.'

Savage circled around to get a better look at him, fascinated by the man's fortitude, and apparent apathy. From behind the bar, Roy tentatively poked up his head.

Without taking his eyes from Vandal, Savage asked Roy, 'Have you got a sawn-off under the counter?'

Roy nodded vigorously. 'Y — Yes, yes I have.'

'Get it out and cover my back,' Savage ordered him. 'Do you think you can do that?'

'S — Sure.'

'Do it then.'

'So, what now?' Vandal sneered at Savage. 'You shoot me down where I sit. Murder me like you did my son?'

Savage opened his mouth to speak but Vandal cut him off.

'Don't tell me you didn't kill him,' he said harshly. 'You may not have pulled the trigger but if you hadn't interfered, he would still be alive.'

Savage ignored him.

Vandal nodded. 'Nothing to say. Well, you didn't answer my question. Maybe we could have a trial. What do you think? Oops, I forgot. The judge kind of lost his head. Come on murderer, what are you going to *do*?'

I'm goin' to blow your damned brains all over this room is what I aim to do.

Savage motioned with the rifle. 'Get up.'

'I don't believe I will,' Vandal told him, with a shake of his head.

'Get up or I'll put a bullet in you,' Savage warned him.

'I don't believe you will,' Vandal said. 'You're the law.'

A cold smile split Savage's lips. *If you only knew.*

The Yellow Boy came up and the dark circle of its gaping maw pressed against Vandal's head. 'Get up.'

Through clenched teeth, Vandal snarled, 'Do it. Go on, kill me.'

A commotion at the front door was greeted by the throaty roar of the shotgun in Roy's hands. The charge of buckshot hammered into the wall above the entry, making the men who were trying to enter, turn tail and run.

The disturbance made Savage whirl about and bring the rifle to bear on the doorway. He realized his mistake immediately and quickly turned back. Seizing the moment, Craig Vandal brought his gun from inside his jacket. The hammer went back as he took aim at the man responsible for the death of his son.

Savage knew that he was a fraction too late, so he lunged to his left in a desperate move to throw off the would-be killer's aim.

The six-gun spat fire and the bullet burned the air close to Savage's face. A snarl of rage came from Vandal's lips when he saw that he'd missed. He tried to sight on his target again but Savage had disappeared behind a nearby table.

He fired twice in frustration and the bullets ripped splinters from the table-top. Cursing, Vandal stepped forward and grasped the edge of the table, ripping it recklessly aside so he could get at Savage.

The Drifter was ready for him. He lay on his back and needed only to raise the rifle and fire. Vandal became aware of his mistake a moment before the .44 Henry slug blew a large hole in his skull.

Savage climbed slowly to his feet. There was a dull throb in his left shoulder where he'd dived on the floor and landed awkwardly. Vandal lay with his eyes open, his body slightly twisted to one side where he'd fallen in a heap.

'Go and join your son,' Savage murmured. 'And be damned.'

'Are you OK, sheriff . . . deputy?' Roy asked.

'Yeah, I'll be fine,' Savage winced.

'You're wounded,' Roy said, indicating his back.

'It's not much,' Savage dismissed his concern.

'I'll get one of the girls to look at it for you,' he persisted. 'Sit down, before you fall down.'

The culmination of everything he'd been through over the last week became too much and Savage felt an overwhelming weariness descend upon him. He thought that Roy's advice might be worth following so he pulled a chair close and sat down. Looking across at the barkeep he said, 'Get me a drink. A big one.'

15

The following dawn was cold and clear after the storm, and as the sun quickly brightened the surrounding landscape, the heavy scent of burnt green timber hung thick in the air. There were still puddles from the downpour the day before, and deep muddy tracks along the street.

An hour after dawn had broken, the undertaker managed to retrieve the charred remains of Malavai from the ruins of the jail, with Savage's supervision. The other bodies, including the head and headless corpse of Judge Perry McArdle, were removed from the street by several men who had tended the wounded the night before.

For such a small town, it had witnessed too much death. Mostly brought about by a young man who believed he was untouchable and a father with blinders, oblivious to his shortcomings.

Savage was packing his saddlebags when a large, well-dressed man found him.

'Mr. Savage, do you have a moment?'

The Drifter was tired and he still hurt from everything that had happened, but he decided to give the man what he asked for. 'Speak while I'm getting ready to leave.'

'That's what I wanted to talk to you about,' the man offered. 'My name is Meyers. Ralph Meyers.'

Savage stopped what he was doing and looked at him square on. He was a middle-aged man with brown hair that was graying at the sides.

'What about me leavin' do you want to know, Mr. Meyers?'

'I — rather, we, were wondering if you would be prepared to stay?' Meyers looked at the badge sitting on the bed. 'Maybe be our new sheriff? We'll need one with Charley gone.'

Savage shook his head. 'I'm leavin'

today. I'm ridin' for Albuquerque.'

'We would pay you well,' Meyers said, trying to change Savage's mind.

Again, the Drifter shook his head. 'No. You can do one thing for me though.'

Although disappointed, Meyers nodded. 'Name it. After all, the town does owe you something for what you did for us.'

'Over in Bad Tooth, there is a woman by the name of Connie,' Savage explained. 'She helped me out when I needed it. Her brother died in the jail last night. Can you send someone over there to tell her?'

'It's not something you would rather do yourself?' Meyers asked.

'Not particularly. The last time I was there I had a few problems with the locals.'

'OK. I'll have someone take care of it.'

A sharp knock at the door drew their attention, and Roy from the saloon appeared, a worried expression on his face.

'What is it, Roy?' Meyers asked before Savage could speak.

'He's back,' Roy said, excitedly.

'Who?'

'The killer,' he told them. 'Rawhide Allen.'

Meyers shifted his gaze and looked at Savage. 'He'll be after you.'

'He ain't alone either,' Roy said. 'He's got a woman along with him.'

A sense of dread filled Savage. 'What does the woman look like?'

'She was — is a — looks, I mean, like a Negro.'

'Damn it,' Savage sighed. 'It don't ever end.'

He grabbed the Yellow Boy from the bed and started for the door.

'Where are you going?' Meyers called after him.

'To finish this,' Savage said angrily.

Outside in the street, he saw the killer and the woman, sitting atop their horses, staring at the pile of burned rubble that had once been the jail.

'Hey!' Savage called out. 'Are you

lookin' for me?'

The man appeared to hip in the saddle but stiffened before he'd got halfway. Instead, he turned the horse, trailing the second horse and Connie, and rode over to where Savage stood.

The first thing that struck the Drifter was the worn and battered look of the woman. She'd obviously had a tough time of it. The second was the way the killer looked. His pallor, his sunken eyes, and hollow cheeks indicated that the man was grievously hurt.

'You'd be Savage,' he rasped. 'You're a hard man to find.'

Allen coughed, a wet, hacking sound that seemed to take all his strength. His wounds were finally getting the better of him. He decided, however, that he had at least one more kill in him.

'You ain't doin' so well, Allen,' Savage observed. 'The man who hired you to kill me is dead. Why don't you let the woman go and get the doc to have a look at you?'

'Give me time to get down off this

horse and we'll see how well I am.'

'Didn't you hear me? I said the man who hired you is dead. There's no need to continue.'

'I took money from him. I'll finish the job.'

Savage cast a glance at Connie. 'Are you OK?'

She nodded. 'I'll live.'

With a pained groan, Allen climbed down from the horse and staggered about like a drunk until he regained control of his feet. A slight breeze sprang up and carried the scent of decay to Savage's nostrils which explained why the killer was the way he was.

'What happened?' Savage asked, hoping to distract Allen from his task.

'Damn Apaches,' he answered. 'One of the bastards shot me. Oh, and the woman stuck me with a knife. Neat trick it was too.'

He coughed again as he moved away from his horse.

'You don't need to do this,' Savage persisted.

'Yeah, I do,' Allen said, and went for his gun.

The weapon never even left its holster. As soon as Allen's hand touched his gun-butt, a coughing fit overcame him. This one would not be stopped and his body convulsed violently with the spasms.

The Yellow Boy in Savage's hands remained silent as he watched and waited for Allen to continue his attempt. Allen seemed to regain his breath, composed himself, looked at Savage and was ready to continue when he fell flat on his face and never moved.

Savage walked over to the prostrate form and squatted next to him. He checked the killer for signs of life but found none.

'Is the son of a bitch dead?' Connie asked.

Savage looked up at her. 'Yeah. He's dead.'

He saw the relief flood through her. 'Thank God.'

The Drifter stood up and walked

over to her horse and started to help her down. While he did, Connie looked about and asked, 'Where's Malavai?'

Savage looked at her hesitantly before saying, 'I need to talk to you about your brother, Connie.'

* * *

The two of them stood beside an open grave in the late afternoon much as Craig Vandal had done only two days before. Only this time it wasn't raining. Connie wept silently as Savage stood beside her, holding his hat in his right hand.

When the preacher was finished, they remained for a while before turning and walking back towards Dead Man's Gulch.

'What do you aim to do now?' Connie asked him, as they ambled along.

'I'll be leavin' tomorrow,' Savage told her.

'And go where?'

'Albuquerque, then further north,' he told her.

'Would you take me with you?' Connie asked, grasping his arm.

Savage patted her on the hand. 'You can't come with me, Connie. I'm not a good man to be around.'

'You seem fine to me,' she protested.

'You don't understand,' he told her. 'Things happen when I'm around. When I was finished with the war, I thought that all the killin' was over. Done with. But ever since, killin' is all I seem to be doin'. No, you are safer away from me.'

There was genuine sadness in her eyes at his refusal, but after a moment she composed herself and said, 'OK then, how about we have dinner tonight before you leave?'

'I'd like that,' he said.

'Good, 'cause you're buyin'. I ain't got squat.'

'I think I can manage that,' Savage laughed.

Connie smiled. The first time since

the news of her brother's death. She hooked her arm through his and said, 'C'mon, you can buy me a drink too.'

The following morning, as Savage was riding the pinto out of Dead Man's Gulch, Connie stretched out her naked form in a large double-bed. Her hands went up under her pillow and bumped something hard. She frowned, still half asleep, rolled over and moved the pillow to see what was there.

When Connie saw it, she had to blink a couple of times to clear her sleep blurred vision. She rolled onto her back and sat up, the sheet falling away to reveal her lithe form. In her hand, was a bundle of paper money. When she counted it later, the amount would come to almost three hundred dollars.

Connie stared at the rumpled sheet beside her and over at the hotel room window, a distant look in her eyes. Then she sighed and said, 'Goodbye, Jeff Savage.'